subculture

by Steve Yockey

A SAMUEL FRENCH ACTING EDITION

SAMUEL FRENCH

FOUNDED 1830

NEW YORK HOLLYWOOD LONDON TORONTO

SAMUELFRENCH.COM

ISBN 978-0-573-69798-2   Printed in U.S.A.   #29274

MUSIC USE NOTE

Licensees are solely responsible for obtaining formal written permission from copyright owners to use copyrighted music in the performance of this play and are strongly cautioned to do so. If no such permission is obtained by the licensee, then the licensee must use only original music that the licensee owns and controls. Licensees are solely responsible and liable for all music clearances and shall indemnify the copyright owners of the play and their licensing agent, Samuel French, Inc., against any costs, expenses, losses and liabilities arising from the use of music by licensees.

IMPORTANT BILLING AND CREDIT
REQUIREMENTS

All producers of *SUBCULTURE must* give credit to the Author of the Play in all programs distributed in connection with performances of the Play, and in all instances in which the title of the Play appears for the purposes of advertising, publicizing or otherwise exploiting the Play and/or a production. The name of the Author *must* appear on a separate line on which no other name appears, immediately following the title and *must* appear in size of type not less than fifty percent of the size of the title type.

contents

[every little thing]

[every little thing] was commissioned by Lisa Paulsen at Emory University's Playwriting Center in Atlanta, Georgia. It appeared as a part of the Spitting Game project in Emory's Brave New Works Festival on February 14, 2009. Directed by Snehal Desai. With the following cast:

DAVID. . . . . Greg Lockett
STEPHANIE. . . . . Chelsea Kaplan
JIMMY . . . . Alec Fox
WOMAN. . . . . .Ellen McQueen

LIST OF PLAYERS

DAVID – a painfully 'visually oriented' young man, hipster, bed head, jeans and a T-shirt.

STEPHANIE – a sensible young woman, very, very put together, sleek, high heels and lipstick.

JIMMY – a frustrated young man on the prowl, tired, idealistic, better looking than he thinks.

WOMAN – a woman, a bit older, relaxed, confident; like a bittersweet reminder of an easier time.

NOTES

[ ] in the script indicate overlapping dialogue.

Everything up to and including the Woman's monologue is direct address to the audience; very isolated, a bit "Brechtian" if you will. Everything after is starkly human.

Projections play across the actors during everything up to the Woman's monologue: a mash-up of pornography, runway, teen dramas, romantic comedies and a collage of Internet chats. The projections stop abruptly before the Woman begins speaking.

Fast, faster, fastest – monologue – release.

(Three people in their early twenties stand in a row facing the audience. A fourth person, a somewhat older woman, sits in a chair nearby casually watching.)

(The projections begin.)

(The three people breath in and then out. Again, they breath in and then out. A third time, in and then…)

JIMMY. So here's the thing, I'm officially boycotting the Internet. Boycott.

STEPHANIE. We're going out tonight, some of my girl-friends I mean, and me, I mean of course I'm going too, I'm part of 'we.'

DAVID. Say what you will, I'm a fan of pornography. People. Having sex. On screen. I fucking love it.

JIMMY. Hear this: I have been on exactly 17 first dates in the last two months, all guys from the internet. All liars.

STEPHANIE. And we all, all of the girls, we sort of call or text to pre-plan what we're going to wear [when we go out.]

DAVID. [I wanna' say the idea of] it is really what gets me, but that's not it.

JIMMY. I'd rather sit at home and play "Candyland" with myself than go on one more first date with some dick I met online.

STEPHANIE. Not like coordinating, but, just getting every-one on the same page. Do you know?

DAVID. My girlfriend, huh, she got all weird about it. She says she's not coming over anymore. Just because, okay, just because I like to have it on when we, well when we fuck, ya' know?

JIMMY. Listen, I think it's great that there is this fast, mass, massive way for people to meet that might never have met in this "thing" called the real world, to get together, but mark my words: trouble.

STEPHANIE. Because the worst thing in the world is when you dress casually and everyone else is dressed to impress. Which has happened, and I don't like that. I don't like it.

JIMMY. This is me on my soap box: A shiny new brand of dishonesty is being bread out there, a symptom of easy [anonymity.]

DAVID. [I know guys are a] lot more visual than women, but she doesn't want to hear that. She doesn't want me to watch it. Not at all. Just the two of us, that should be [enough. Whatever.]

STEPHANIE. [One time I] showed up at this bar in jeans and a shirt, hair just kinda', ugh, my friends were all wearing skirts, looking very good, and, I mean, not a guy there looked at me all night. You've heard the one about the three girls who walk into a bar? Two of the girls a pretty and one of them, well, isn't or whatever, and the bartender says, ugh, I don't know why I'm, I don't even like that joke.

JIMMY. Think about [this...]

STEPHANIE. [I am] that joke. Was [that...]

JIMMY. [When you're] talking to someone online, they have time to think about how to respond, they have time to craft a response, to look things up for reference, to change, to figure out how best to offer you what you're looking for, to become that thing. Tricky.

DAVID. When I'm watching really hot porn, it's, there's something in it that makes me feel closer, and obviously more, something that really just gets me, uh, up and running.

STEPHANIE. So that night out, it was bizarre because when we all dress the same, I get attention. I don't want to sound, I don't care how it sounds, I get attention from guys. That I like.

JIMMY. Scary. Not just the Internet, texting too, this rapid fire transaction. Who is on the other side of it? Who's that guy anyway? A lot of the time, you don't [really know.]

DAVID. [And it's not] like I need it or anything, I don't have to have porn to, ya' know, perform or whatever. And she knows that. I used to never watch it, then a little. I do watch [it more now.]

JIMMY. [I'm no Luddite, but] things are moving just a little too fast when you chat with someone so much online that you think you're in love only to meet them face to face and [have nothing to say.]

STEPHANIE. [And it's not like] anyone did anything on purpose, I mean, I'm making it a bigger deal than it is, was, I could have gone home, but being in for one night just because I didn't look like, well, whatever the rest of that sentence [is I guess.]

DAVID. [She doesn't] get that the videos [make it so much better, I get harder, seriously, so fucking hard.]

STEPHANIE. [But I vividly remember, vividly, the way that I was outside of] the, [what, the group.]

JIMMY. [How are] you gonna' sit across from me at dinner after we have talked online about the virtues and wonders of *The Great Gatsby* and tell me, face to face, you don't know anything about F. Scott Fitzgerald? He wrote it.

DAVID. And, okay, maybe she can go, sure, it's like, the sex is almost better when she's not there, between you and me.

STEPHANIE. And one of those guys [that night...]

DAVID. [Strictly between] you and me.

STEPHANIE. He said what's with your "boring" friend? About me he said that. Like I'm waiting in the corner at a sock hop for someone to ask me to dance. And you know, you just know what "boring" really [means.]

JIMMY. [We're having] dinner, drinks, conversation and every little fake thing is peeling away.

STEPHANIE. [It doesn't] [mean "boring."]

DAVID. [I've never really] [thought about it.]

JIMMY. [Every little bit] [of his game.]

STEPHANIE. [And the worst] thing, I didn't even know him, but it felt so, look, I know I look good. I just wasn't dressed, up, or whatever.

DAVID. *(laughing to himself…)* The sex is better when she's not there.

STEPHANIE. Oh god.

JIMMY. Oh god.

DAVID. Oh my god.

STEPHANIE. And so, lesson learned, I realized something very important. I can control never having to feel like that again. And it's simple. Look better than my friends.

(STEPHANIE self-consciously adjusts her appearance.)

JIMMY. That is incorrect. To sit there and lie about yourself. You don't have to be smart, I'm not saying you have to be smart. Just not stupid. And more importantly, be in real life whoever you were when we were talking online. Jesus, it's like Los Angeles is taking over the world, and I don't mean Los Angeles, I mean the idea that you have in your head when I say "Los Angeles." It's in there, you know what I mean.

DAVID. When I'm watching a good video, really getting into it, I don't even imagine anything, [fantasize, I can sit back, take things at my own speed. Really get into it. And not think. Just watch the video go by and my body responds. I don't even pay a lot of attention to what I'm doing, ya' know, physically, to myself. It feels good, but my brain kinda' hangs there, disconnected, and this base kind of thing just, just…]

STEPHANIE. [And so I lost 10 pounds, which maybe I didn't need to do, but it felt like doing something, and bought some new clothes and realized, boom, [[just like that: if I can get my friends to text me photos of what they're wearing out, I can do just a little more. Maybe not enough to notice, but enough for guys to notice.] Which, frankly, doesn't take much if it means shorter, tighter or a bit more, I don't know, just a bit more.]]

JIMMY. [[My heart, all right, my heart cannot take anymore of this artifice and inflation. I admit that I am at a loss sometimes when it comes to dealing with people and the internet makes it easier, but how many times do I have to go through the same horribly deflating let down as whatever's been built up in an unseen]] [void is slowly torn down piece by piece by the real life incarnation that can't live up to the invention.

DAVID. [I'm not even there, not even involved, just a body, I'm gone inside these women on the screen, my cock in my hand, everything on] [the inside of my chest just pulls up, collapsing, like it's being sucked out through the back of my neck and I hear my own breath.]

STEPHANIE. [And all of the girls were willing to do it,] [it was so easy because it seemed fun.]

JIMMY. [So what am I] [supposed to do?]

DAVID. [And pause this part of the tape, the] best part, all my muscles tense up, [my body rigid and stuff.]

STEPHANIE. [So I always cheat a bit more,] I can't help it, [the attention just, just feels so good.]

DAVID. [And everything gets faster, my breathing,] [the rhythm with my hand…]

JIMMY. [You have to play the game,] go through the, jump [through the hoops.]

STEPHANIE. [And no one's] gonna' [ignore me.]

DAVID. [My heartbeat,] [faster.]

JIMMY. [Fucking hoop] [after hoop.]

STEPHANIE. [And no one's gonna'] [call me names.]

DAVID. [And slippery,] [mm, yes.]

STEPHANIE. [Because I know how] [to look good.]

DAVID. [Yes. Yes.]

STEPHANIE. [I look good.]

DAVID. But [it feels so good. So fucking good.]

STEPHANIE. [But then I catch myself] [in the mirror and…]

JIMMY. [What choice do] [I have?]

DAVID. [Ah fuck yes!]

(The projections stop. **JIMMY** *looks away, annoyed.*
STEPHANIE *stares ahead, eyes wide.* **DAVID***'s breathing
is fast and erratic. It slows and calms during the following. As the* **WOMAN** *speaks, the attention of the other
three is drawn to her...)*

WOMAN. This summer I spent some time in India. I travel a
lot, so I don't often have those 'culture shock' moments.
A city is a city, all that, cell phones, traffic, noise. The
people are different, that's all. But one afternoon, my
car, and I use that term as loosely as possible, my car
broke down on a rural stretch of road. And I was angry.
Just angry. No one wants to hang around a dirt highway,
in the heat, waiting for rescue in the indefinite future,
especially when you don't speak the language. And my
computer battery was dead so I couldn't even get any
work done. Just really frustrating. But while I'm sitting
there in the middle of nowhere, no cell reception, no
nothing, I'm absentmindedly fiddling with my wedding ring, which I do when I get nervous, just twisting it
around and around and I look up...I see an elephant.
An elephant. Just standing there, a real elephant, big,
too, bigger than you'd think from the movies. I've
never been to a zoo, not since I was a kid anyway, and
I'm not an animal lover, but there was something so,
I don't know, I just kinda' stopped. Stood there, staring. A real elephant on the side of the road. I basically
ignored my driver and walked over, but it didn't move.
I slowly reached out and it still didn't move, but one of
its big eyes followed my hand all the way until I touched
its trunk. It was coarse and leathery as I rubbed up and
down. Then the elephant flapped its ears some, lifted
up its trunk and gently wrapped it around my shoulder.
My driver said something in Hindi, but he sounded
miles away. I looked right in the elephants' eye and it
looked back at me. This huge animal, this thing I've
seen on television or in movies more times than I can
count, was touching me, seeing me. And I looked at my
hand against its head. My wedding ring in clear relief
against the gray.

(She holds out her hand examining her ring, a sweet admiration.)

WOMAN. *(cont.)* And, as silly as this sounds, I saw my husband, but the way he was when we first met. When he asked me out after an English seminar in college. How he held my hand that first night and I didn't know anything about him and I wanted to know everything about him, but we had barely spoken and there was so much to learn. And we had so much time to learn it all. I swear, I swear that was the most intensely real moment that has ever happened. I just started crying, in a good way, I can't even tell you why. I think about it all the time. It's just in there, that memory, waiting for any quiet moment to take hold. An elephant on the side of the road in India. An innocence that maybe doesn't exist anymore. Maybe never really existed. Oh that's awful, but what if it never really was as gorgeously uncomplicated as I remember. But I like to think it was.

(She looks at the three of them for the first time since launching into her story.)

When it's quiet, I like to think people can still connect like that.

(Pause. All of the characters breath out of sequence, but slowly and obviously they all come into sequence with the Women's breathing pattern. They also now see each other, are aware of and hear each other, speak to each other.)

(DAVID shakes out his hand...)

DAVID. And once I'm done, catch my breath, look at the screen...and it's different. That image of a woman being, frozen, seems a little duller, less fantastic. Kinda' plain. It'll look better again, when I need it to look better, but right now, spent, maybe I can really see it. It's not sexy. It's just sex. A picture of sex. And it's far away. This is the part where someone else would touch you and you'd feel something. That's not happening.

STEPHANIE. But when I look at myself in the mirror, before I go out for, where ever, I feel this gnawing thing. It's not guilt or whatever, I mean, it's not that. But I look at myself and think, does all of this make me pretty? Am I pretty? Or just better sport.

JIMMY. The other thing that sits with you, is this awful hope that even though there's a lot more information, opportunity to lie, the right person might be one click away. [One click.]

STEPHANIE. [Because] you have to do something, to, to compete, I [don't know.]

JIMMY. [And that's] a tough hope to throw [away.]

DAVID. [And if] she doesn't come back, is this all I've got?

STEPHANIE. That sounds so…

JIMMY. Oh god.

STEPHANIE. Oh god.

DAVID. Oh my god.

JIMMY. So I guess I'll keep looking.

DAVID. Alone. Watching. Just [watching.]

STEPHANIE. [I mean, look,] we all do what we can, even if none of it's…

End of Play

sucker punch

sucker punch was commissioned and produced by Dad's Garage Theatre Company in Atlanta, GA. It opened on January 20, 2007 as a part of *8½ x 11: Sex, Drugs and Rock 'n Roll*. Directed by Mike Katinsky. With the following cast:

MAGGIE... Eve Krueger
DARLA ....Lauren Gunderson
MR. SANDERS..................................John Benzinger

LIST OF PLAYERS

MAGGIE: a woman in her 20s, all business, all the time
DARLA: a woman in her 20s, childlike, raging, confused
MR. SANDERS: a man in his 40s, caught and anxious to deal

NOTES

[ ] indicates overlapping dialogue

The setting for the play need be nothing more than a couch, or even the idea of a couch.

The handgun should be as large and imposing as possible, even cartoonish.

The entire pace should move quickly; fast and rollicking. But Darla's final monologue should spin into something fleeting, lifted, something else all together.

(From darkness, two women are mid-conversation, very tense.)

(During the following exchange, a spot light grows illuminating only **MR. SANDERS**. *In the middle of the floor, he is bent over on his knees unconscious. He is in his underwear, gagged with his hands tied behind his back. A fit man, he is bleeding from the head.)*

MAGGIE. Where are you going!

DARLA. You, you saw him, he was being crazy, he's crazy. I'm outta' here.

MAGGIE. Calm down Darla, we don't have the money yet.

DARLA. He hit me, nobody fucking hits me Maggie. Not anymore.

MAGGIE. He's under control now.

DARLA. You even don't care, do you? You're in there doing your [nails.]

MAGGIE. [We can't] leave without the money.

DARLA. You're just like Mom.

MAGGIE. What does, what? Don't talk to me like [that, Darla.]

DARLA. [Quit telling] me what to do! You always [do that!]

MAGGIE. [Shut-up!]

(The light slowly spreads out to envelope the entire stage. **MAGGIE** *and* **DARLA**, *two attractive women, stand together near a couch in a hotel room. They are both in sexy outfits, short skirts, high heels, very provocative.* **DARLA** *chews gum, smacking. She has a black eye.)*

DARLA. At least you used to check in and make sure everything was okay. Now you just wait outside. I mean I'm hoppin' around in here all by myself with this guy. He could've killed me.

MAGGIE. Stop being so fucking dramatic.

DARLA. Look at my face, look what he did. I'm not... he's waking up.

MAGGIE. I'm serious Darla, don't make [such a...]

DARLA. [He's waking] up.

(**MR. SANDERS** *mumbles. They just look at him.*)

MAGGIE. Okay, just play it cool, okay? We'll leave soon, okay? Just let me get what we deserve.

DARLA. I don't even... fine.

(*He screams something unintelligible through the gag.*)

MAGGIE. Welcome back sleepy head.

(**MAGGIE** *crosses to him, removing his gag.*)

DARLA. Tell him to be nice. And not to talk with his mouth full.

MR. SANDERS. What the fuck are you doing!? How long are you gonna' keep me like this! Do you have [any idea...]

DARLA. [Tell him] to quit yelling!

MAGGIE. Quit yelling or I'll hit you again.

MR. SANDERS. No, no, no, I'm sorry, I'm sorry. Just, just untie me.

DARLA. No!

MAGGIE. I'm not sure I should do that after your little outburst earlier. Your little behavioral [aberration.]

MR. SANDERS. [Look, I] know, I know I lost control. I'm sorry if I scared you, I didn't mean to break anything. You [won't...]

MAGGIE. [Are] you under the impression that we care if you bust up this fancy hotel suite?

MR. SANDERS. I thought [you...]

MAGGIE. [That was] rhetorical Mr. Sanders as we don't give a good god damn about your room, it's your room, now let me tell you where the issue began: you paid for the basic package. I'm not sure if that's because you are cheap, poor, uncertain, a jerk, a novice or any combination of the above; however, the basic package does not include abuse. And when you punched Darla in the face, well that [was...]

MR. SANDERS. [You've] got to be joking, [right?]

MAGGIE. [I'm sorry,] what did you [say?]

MR. SANDERS. [You have] no idea what you're doing here, right? Do you know what they do to girls like you in prison?

DARLA. [Yes.]

MAGGIE. [Yes.]

MR. SANDERS. I'm serious!

MAGGIE. And how would that conversation go? "Oh Mr. Policeman, after I paid them to have sex with me, these two women subdued me to stop me from beating them up. Please don't tell my wife."

DARLA. *(sing-songy...)* We found your wedding ring.

MAGGIE. Wife doesn't like the hard stuff?

DARLA. *(still sing-songy...)* We found your gun too.

(**MAGGIE** *produces a large gun and pushes him back hard with her shoe on his chest and squares the gun at him.*)

MAGGIE. Does she like your big [gun?]

DARLA. [Bet you] never hit her when you can't get it up at home!

MR. SANDERS. You're not gonna' shoot me.

MAGGIE. *(slowly trailing the gun down his chest and into the front of his underwear)* Oh really, I'm not?

MR. SANDERS. You couldn't fucking shoot me [if you...]

DARLA. [One more] word and she will shoot you in the back of the head, and if you wiggle around, it won't matter, she's a real good shot, just, bam! She used to practice on rabbits when we were little, and rabbits are fast. Faster than you.

MR. SANDERS. Jesus, it's not even loaded.

(**MAGGIE** *and* **DARLA** *exchange a glance.* **MAGGIE** *pulls* *the trigger with the gun still at* **MR. SANDERS** *' waist. It clicks with a hollow noise.)*

MAGGIE. Damn it.

(**MR. SANDERS** *laughs and* **MAGGIE** *hits him with the gun.)*

DARLA. Hit him again!

MAGGIE. *(tossing the gun on the floor in disappointment)* All right Mr. Sanders, clearly threatening you with an empty gun isn't going to get us anywhere.

DARLA. And we can't find your money. I'm mean we've looked [everywhere.]

MAGGIE. [Shut-up!]

DARLA. What?

MR. SANDERS. Fuck you. I'll beat the shit out of you.

MAGGIE. Aw, you like hitting girls?

MR. SANDERS. Fuck you.

MAGGIE. You like hitting girls?

MR. SANDERS. So the fuck what!

MAGGIE. You're getting pretty angry, huh? Okay…

(A moment of reflection, then…)

Okay, look, this is a business agreement and it doesn't need to get antagonistic. You have a need and we want payment, it's all terms now, right? Mr. Sanders, you booked the basic package, which you got. And I'm sorry that you couldn't… 'complete the transaction.' But you don't get to hit Darla. That's only available in the advanced package. The more expensive selection. You've got 18 minutes left, so just [tell me…]

MR. SANDERS. [Are you,] so, so wait, if I pay more, I can hit you? How much to hit [you?]

MAGGIE. [Now pay] attention, you can't hit me. But for the right price, Darla is another [story.]

DARLA. [I don't] want to get hit, what are you [doing?]

MR. SANDERS. [How much?] Then how much for some

more coke and some quality time with her?

MAGGIE. Is there more coke?

DARLA. Sometimes I feel like I might as well not talk at all, like maybe I'm a little bunny rabbit. Like somewhere inside me I have floppy ears and a little tail.

MAGGIE. Darla.

DARLA. It's in your purse, but the coke is why he couldn't 'complete the transaction' in the first place. Tell him he shouldn't do other people's drugs, that's not okay!

MAGGIE. Darla.

DARLA. Stop talking to me like a little kid Maggie. Every time: "Darla." "Darla."

MAGGIE. We can talk about this later, when Mr. Sanders is finished.

DARLA. "We can talk about this later…"

MAGGIE. God! What is wrong with you tonight?

DARLA. Nothing. I'm sweet and adorable, like a little bunny.

(She sits, crossing her arms, looking away.)

MAGGIE. Not the fucking bunny thing Darla, Jesus Christ.

MR. SANDERS. I don't care about the fucking coke, that's okay, just, I'll pay you whatever, just leave me alone with her. Oh my God leave me alone with her. How much? $300, $400?

MAGGIE. Whaddya' think Darla?

DARLA. I think I'd be a soft, white bunny, with a little pink nose.

MAGGIE. Darla! Whaddya' think about his offer?

DARLA. His offer?

MAGGIE. His offer.

DARLA. I'm serious, stop playing around. My face already hurts.

MAGGIE. That's so sweet. Darla suffers from an intense case of low self-esteem. It's sad really, I try to tell her how special she is, but she tends not to know what she's worth.

(She gingerly rubs her hand along **DARLA***'s cheek.)*

A beautiful face like this, she can't let you mess it up for a pittance like $400. I mean, we're gonna' be out of work for at least a few days while she heals up. How would we manage? So I would think $1,000 would get you what you're asking for now. $1,000 for your last 13 minutes. How does that sound?

MR. SANDERS. You said 18 minutes!

MAGGIE. Well all this negotiating, I mean tick tock. And you'll tire yourself out pretty quick I'd [imagine.]

MR. SANDERS. [I, I don't,] fuck, I don't have that much.

MAGGIE. Mr. Sanders, I must confess to some minor confusion on my part. Did you perhaps take us for inexpensive dates?

DARLA. We're not cheap!

MAGGIE. That's right, we're upscale. Decidedly [upscale...]

DARLA. [I'm not] cheap you son of a bitch!

MR. SANDERS. That's right, just keep screaming at me. I'm gonna' hurt you like you can't imagine.

DARLA. Wrong!

MAGGIE. Not if you can't pay the price.

MR. SANDERS. All right, okay, I can pay it, I've got it, I'll pay it.

MAGGIE. *(trying to cover her surprise)* The full $1,000?

MR. SANDERS. Yes. Yes! Only after, you can have it after. Every single cent. After.

DARLA. *(pulling a triumphant* **MAGGIE** *aside, quickly, quietly...)* I thought you were playing him, are you being serious? I can't do that, why would you, are you serious?

MAGGIE. I love you honey, but business is business. And this is our business.

DARLA. Business is...this isn't charging for me to make out with boys behind the movie theater, this isn't even selling me for sex. This is some other kinda', and you don't even know if he really has the money! Look at me; I don't want to do this.

MAGGIE. But what if he does have it? Think about it; it'll only hurt a little and you're getting half of $1,000. We can take some time off with that much.

DARLA. Only hurt a little?

MR. SANDERS. Oh it's gonna' hurt more than a little.

MAGGIE. You're not helping.

DARLA. I won't do it.

MAGGIE. Look, you're gonna' do it okay? I don't know where this newfound prudishness has come [from, but...]

DARLA. [Prudishness!?] You want to let him beat me for money.

MAGGIE. You've done everything else?

DARLA. Uh! Sex stuff, not, not this. And only because you said it's the only thing we can do, or else we have to go back to Kansas. I'm not going back there. But this is, is why we left in the [first place!]

MAGGIE. [That's right.] And haven't I looked out for you?

DARLA. But I'm always the one who has to do the, the "things." Why not you? You do it! Why me and not [you?]

MAGGIE. [That's] ridiculous, why would it be me? I've always carried you around. I brought you here with me. I saved you; you owe me and I want this money.

DARLA. I'm not a punching bag!

MAGGIE. Don't be stupid! I'm tired of talking. Especially in front of some guy we don't even know that you tied up.

DARLA. You're the one that hit him! Twice!

MAGGIE. To help you!

MR. SANDERS. Fuck, this is ridiculous. This would be funny if it wasn't so fucked up.

MAGGIE. [Shut-up!]

DARLA. [Shut-up!]

MAGGIE. You know, think of it like this… Dad used to beat you, a lot, and okay, that's not fair,

DARLA. You always hid in the pantry, locked me out when he was angry.

MAGGIE. Well I didn't want to get hit! We couldn't both hide in there; he would have found us both. But listen, this guy is willing to pay for it. You're already used to it right?

(**DARLA** *tries to pull away, but* **MAGGIE** *grabs her arm…*)

So really it won't be so bad. And it will help us. And we probably won't have to do it again anytime soon. Darla, every moment we have together now, away from how things were back home, every moment is precious. Think of it that way, like a little sacrifice…so we can be happy.

DARLA. That's a really… pretty thought Maggie.

MAGGIE. And it's a lot of money. And I want it. You're gonna' do this, right honey?

DARLA. You're really gonna' make me?

MAGGIE. Yes.

(*Pause. During the passage, a hot white glow light grows on* **DARLA.**)

DARLA. Can we do some more coke first? It'll help me hold still better. And I can think of other things, it helps me think of other things. Like when we snuck into that Heart concert when we were little, before they got all soft-rock, when they were still hard and we drove all the way into the city, to that club and everyone was sweaty and pushing together and we did coke for the first time, from that guy with the gloves with no fingers and I couldn't move and Anne and Nancy Wilson were so amazing and they were sisters just like us and so strong and we thought we could do anything if we could just get out of that fucking town and I'll only do a little, just a little, I promise, but then I can close my eyes and sometimes I feel like I'm in a crowd of people, no, a big field, one with tall grass, like back home but nicer, grass all the way up to here and it's brushing on my fingers, like I could run my hands around in circles and feel it on my palms, or if I were a little bunny, then I'd be so small; I'd just disappear into the field, be swallowed up the people and the grass and the music and go away, all alone, all by myself and maybe I'm not me, if I'm a bunny, and I can hide on my own and I'm not even here at all, when it's like that, I can barely feel a thing.

MAGGIE. Darla?

(The light vanishes abruptly.)

DARLA. Can I do some coke first please?

MAGGIE. Okay, let me find it. You know I can't say no to you. But hurry, okay? Tick tock.

MR. SANDERS. Here we go. Here we go.

*(**MAGGIE** begins to go through her purse. **DARLA** picks up the gun off the floor.)*

DARLA. I love you Maggie.

MAGGIE. I love you too little sis…

*(**DARLA** smashes the gun over the back of **MAGGIE**'s head and she falls to the ground unconscious. She grabs the purse and begins to leave.)*

MR. SANDERS. Wait! Wait! Please untie me, fuck, don't leave me like this. How am I supposed to, don't leave me like this, please, I'll pay you, I'll pay you [whatever you…]

(She hits him in the head with the gun, knocking him to the floor.)

DARLA. [You're fucking] lucky there are no bullets in that gun. Pay her when she wakes up. I'm not a fucking rabbit and I'm not for sale anymore.

(She exits. Blackout.)

End of Play

kiss & tell

kiss & tell premiered at Vital Theater Company in New York, New York as a part of the Vital Signs Festival. It opened on December 6, 2007. Directed by Bob Cline, with the following cast:

BRANDON..Chris Van Hoy
ZACK.. Caleb Damschroder
SUSIE..Rachel Mewbron

LIST OF PLAYERS

BRANDON – a male college student, awkward-cute
ZACK – a male college student, polished, flirty
SUSIE – a female college student, brash, sarcastic

NOTES

[ ] in the script indicate overlapping dialogue.

The entire play takes place in a pool of light. No set pieces, no sound, no props – with the notable exception of a sledgehammer.

(Lights up on a pool of light. **SUSIE** *and* **ZACK** *sit on one side of the light, lounging on the ground.)*

SUSIE. I can't believe we're actually sitting here; we should just go before he comes back.

ZACK. It's fine.

SUSIE. I've never hung out in a tool shed. Did you see the shelves of different drills and saws by the door? What if he's a psycho killer?

ZACK. Oh for fuck's sake, it's not a tool shed, it's, like, a little back house. He just doesn't want his parents to know we're drinking. A lot.

SUSIE. You owe me big for this.

ZACK. He seems so sweet.

SUSIE. Psycho killer.

*(***BRANDON*** *enters.)*

BRANDON. Hey, I checked in the kitchen, there's no more beer left. Sorry.

ZACK. That's okay; let's just get back to the game. Susie, you picked "dare."

SUSIE. Ugh.

ZACK. And I dare you to kiss Brandon.

BRANDON. Um…

SUSIE. That's all?

(She sits up and pulls her hair back. **BRANDON** *laughs.)*

I can do that in my sleep. You ready?

BRANDON. I'm good, I'm okay.

SUSIE. All right, here we go.

(She leans in towards him, eyes closed, provocative. He leans towards her, eyes open, nervous. **ZACK** *lights up and adjusts his position for a better view. Before their*

faces get too close, the moment freezes into a tableau.
BRANDON *tilts his face out a bit, not towards the audience, but removed from the scene.)*

BRANDON. In this moment, there is this strange feeling in the pit of my stomach. I'm trying so hard to hide it, to look really natural about it, so they don't think I'm weird or anything. But this is definitely a new kinda' thing for me. I never really had any friends before, I know how that sounds, but my parents are really, protective, I guess that's the word for it. And college is my, I don't know, my first chance to try and fit in, to try to, I don't know. But it isn't going well, everything's so hard, I don't know how to be around other people, they seem, not like me and I can't make myself fit. But that's, so I have to fake it, to try and figure out how I'm supposed to be. And I meet these two and they're fun, they seem to like me, and we get alcohol and come back to my house, even though we have to hide form my folks. This is what people do, right? A first stab at being, I don't know, normal. Her mouth is so close; I can feel her breath a little. There's all of this kind of anxious tension wrapped around the whole, around everything, dripping off of everything. And our lips meet. There is something cool about it, cold about it, not wet; dry and uncomfortable. Something not right, but I do what I think I'm supposed to do. The whole time I'm staring at a row of screwdrivers hanging on the wall behind her, all different sizes, counting them over and over again. Still [somehow I...]

SUSIE. [I can't] believe how lame [this is.]

ZACK. [She won't] ever really [kiss him.]

BRANDON. [I don't] know how it should feel and so I just...

*(The tableau breaks as **BRANDON** kisses her. Briefly. He then sits back away form her and she is left hanging in the kiss for a moment. She opens her eyes and quickly recovers.)*

SUSIE. See, no big deal.

ZACK. You're blushing.

SUSIE. I'm not!

BRANDON. I don't want to sound; I'm just a little uncomfortable. You guys play this game all the time?

SUSIE. [Not, really.]

ZACK. [Sure we do.]

> *(pause)*

We play it all the time.

BRANDON. All right…okay.

ZACK. We don't usually have to hide in a tool shed though.

BRANDON. Well I mean, we can stay out here and drink or we can go into the main house and not drink with my parents. I don't think you'd like them.

SUSIE. At least it's bigger than my apartment. And only a little creepy.

ZACK. Awww, no. It's just, ya' know…industrial.

BRANDON. My Dad's in heavy construction. I was, I spent time alone a lot as a kid, so I used to play in here all the time.

ZACK. Really?

BRANDON. Sure. I'm pretty familiar with most of the things in here. But just, just don't touch anything. He doesn't come out here much, but he knows where everything in here is supposed to be and he's still got a temper.

ZACK. We won't touch a thing, [I promise.]

SUSIE. [Come on] boys, my turn, it's my turn!

ZACK. This should be interesting.

SUSIE. Truth or dare?

ZACK. Me?

SUSIE. You. Truth. Or. Dare?

ZACK. Dare.

SUSIE. Brilliant, turn about is fair play. I dare you to kiss Brandon.

That's the dare.

ZACK. That's not very cool to rope our host into the dare again, now is it, Susie? You don't care, do you Brandon? It's a silly game. In a fucking tool shed.

SUSIE. Blah, blah, you don't mind, do you Brandon?

ZACK. You don't have to say yes [just because...]

BRANDON. [It's no big] deal, right? A game. I can, I mean, I'll play.

(*Pause.* **ZACK** *smiles.* **BRANDON** *drops his head self-consciously.*)

SUSIE. Perfect.

BRANDON. But I've never really, just, you're not gonna' tell anyone, right?

ZACK. [Wouldn't dream of it.]

SUSIE. [Absolutely not.]

(*She moves from between them.*)

Nothing leaves here.

BRANDON. I guess.

ZACK. Maybe we should drink a little more?

SUSIE. You don't need to drink anymore and we already drank everything.

ZACK. Okay.

BRANDON. Maybe we should just...

(**ZACK** *and* **BRANDON** *awkwardly lean toward each other.* **SUSIE** *watches intently. She positions herself to watch.* **ZACK** *shift a little to block her view. She adjusts again with a smile.* **ZACK** *and* **BRANDON** *both close their eyes. Before their faces get too close, the moment freezes into a tableau.* **ZACK** *tilts his face out a bit, not towards the audience, but removed from the scene.*)

ZACK. In this moment, he is close enough that I can smell him; his cologne or aftershave, whatever, it's intoxicating. Sandlewood and something...something sweet. Maybe vanilla? And his eyes are closed, so I close mine as we drift closer and closer. I've been watching him on campus for a few weeks. Not in a stalker way or anything, but he is really attractive and always by himself for some reason. I could never figure out why, which just adds to the curiosity. When Susie agreed to invite him out, we both new the plan. I was so glad when she agreed to come back to his house too, but now I wish she hadn't. I almost hope that she'll look away, let me have this kind of intimate thing. Of course she doesn't, she wouldn't do that, but I hope for it anyway. And as our lips meet, I think how it's all working out so perfectly. But the contact between our mouths erases everything from my head. This kind of pulse, this pressure that makes me want to press harder. Something I can feel all through my body, my mouth wet from his mouth, his tongue, everything suspended in the air above our heads. My brain is flooded with all of these vaguely romantic ideas that I never let myself. Never let myself...But I can't help it. It's fuzzy and warm, but it all snaps away as soon as we break, still...

SUSIE. This is exactly what Zack [wanted.]

BRANDON. [I've never] felt anything [like this.]

ZACK. [I don't] want it to stop.

(The tableau breaks as they kiss softly, briefly. They pull apart just a little bit, opening their eyes and looking at each other. Then kiss more deeply, intensely. The moment is broken after SUSIE *begins laughing and clapping. They pull apart,* ZACK *pleased,* BRANDON *self-consciously.)*

SUSIE. Good work.

ZACK. Good kiss.

BRANDON. Oh, I don't know, [it was...]

SUSIE. [You really got] into that [one, huh?]

ZACK. [I'll say.]

BRANDON. No, I just got [kinda'...]

SUSIE. [I'm a little] jealous.

ZACK. You should be. I told you I was right.

SUSIE. Zack was so sure you were into guys, but I told him
    you [were just a…]

BRANDON. [I'm not, I'm, I've] never even kissed anyone
    before.

ZACK. Oh come on.

BRANDON. I'm serious.

SUSIE. Oh! I can't wait to tell Jenny, she owes you twenty
    bucks.

ZACK. She's never gonna' believe me. Especially the part
    about the tool shed.

SUSIE. Hey, I'm a witness. I'll [stand up and…]

    (ZACK and SUSIE laugh.)

SUSIE. [Take a] breath [Brandon.]

ZACK. [It's no big] deal man, calm down.

BRANDON. But I only did [it because…]

    (He rushes out of the light.)

SUSIE. [Oh Brandon,] come back!

ZACK. God, what's the problem, he didn't seem to mind
    the kiss?

SUSIE. You know, some guys don't like to admit certain
    things about themselves.

ZACK. You don't really think that was his first kiss, do you?

SUSIE. No. He kissed me first, right?

ZACK. You know what I mean.

SUSIE. We're in college, how could that be his first kiss?
    We're practically grown up for fuck's sake. I mean, I
    was still right that he's kinda'…

    (She makes a gesture for "crazy" with her fingers.)

    He has to hide in his parents' tool shed to drink.

ZACK. You're being a bitch.

SUSIE. I can't believe we got him to kiss you.

ZACK. Don't be mean.

SUSIE. You've got to be kidding.

ZACK. *(touching his lips)* Besides, maybe it was special.

SUSIE. What're you, in love?

> (**BRANDON** *enters again, dragging a large sledgehammer behind him, scraping along the ground. He stops just outside the light.*)

ZACK. Stop it. Brandon? Come back in here man, seriously.

SUSIE. What do you have?

BRANDON. I'm pretty familiar with most of the things in here.

SUSIE. Oh don't be upset, we were just playing a game. Just like [you said.]

BRANDON. [I don't want] you guys to tell, I didn't want. I don't want this to happen.

SUSIE. See, this is what I'm talking about.

> *(She whispers...)*

Crazy.

ZACK. We were just saying, it can't really be your first kiss, right?

BRANDON. *(very quiet)* It was my first kiss.

ZACK. Why would anyone wait that long?

SUSIE. Well, maybe an ugly person, but you're a good-looking guy. Bizarre, but good-looking.

ZACK. Really good-looking.

SUSIE. Or we wouldn't have picked you to play in the [first place.]

> *(They begin laughing again.* **BRANDON** *lunges into the light.)*

BRANDON. [It's not] funny!

> *(He rears back the hammer, about to bring it down towards* **ZACK.** **ZACK** *starts to turn towards* **BRANDON,** *a smile still on his face.* **SUSIE** *leans back, hands on the floor. The moment freezes into a tableau.* **SUSIE** *tilts her face out a bit, not towards the audience, but removed from the scene.)*

SUSIE. In this moment, Zack is almost looking at me. He has this smile on his face, this amazing smile and I can tell he really likes this guy. It's the only reason I agreed to the stupid game in the first place. The sound that Brandon makes when he starts to swing the, the hammer, the sound of the effort, it catches Zack's attention. He starts to look away from me, look towards Brandon, but his face only makes it about half way before the head of the hammer catches his chin. There is an awful noise, fucking awful, as it just kind of rips his jaw off. It all comes off, almost like it's detachable, like it's supposed to come off. For a minute, everything freezes and there's nothing, like it's not real. But then Zack makes this sound that, that maybe would have been a scream but instead it's this muddled, confused noise from his throat, this gagging noise from the missing bottom half of his face. And then blood starts up, pouring out everywhere, every-where, waves of it spilling out on the floor. He falls over on the floor, trying to make it stop with his hands, looking up at me, eyes pleading, but I don't know what to do, I don't even scream.

I look up at Brandon; he's holding the hammer in both of his hands, breathing really heavy and crying. I feel like I'm looking at him, no, like I see him for the very first time as he pulls the hammer back over his head again. I don't even try to move. My brain is caught in this loop, this one twitch of thought that keeps coming and coming, again and again, I can't think of anything else. He brings the hammer down towards my face with this guttural, animal sound, and the thought is still in my head slamming around behind my eyes, all I can think: it was just a game. I mean...

(BRANDON. *Still holding the hammer poised, struck suddenly by heavy breathing...*)

No one's gonna' know.

ZACK. *(still smiling, speaking over* **BRANDON***'s heavy breathing…)* I don't even feel it, not in a real way, just a cracking noise in my ears and the dark of the tool shed disappearing, my body moving involuntarily, my hands, but I don't see it, only this light pouring into my eyes as they spiral open.

SUSIE. *(looks out into the audience for the first time, tears falling…)* It was only a kiss.

End of Play

dizziness & loss of breath

dizziness & loss of breath was commissioned by Lisa Paulsen at Emory University's Playwriting Center in Atlanta, GA. It appeared as a part of the Spitting Game project in Emory's Brave New Works Festival on February 14, 2009. Directed by Snehal Desai. With the following cast:

SARA. . . . . Camille Bullock
ALISON . . . . Chelsea Kaplan

LIST OF PLAYERS

SARA: a young woman, very practical, still stylish and maybe a bit provocative; a bit hard, but it's a cover

ALISON: a young woman, a little more rough and tumble, not in appearance but in demeanor; somewhat sad

NOTES

[ ] in the script indicate overlapping dialogue.

At the very least, the bass from the music playing downstairs at the party should be audible in the bedroom, a soft blanket around the play. Labored, difficult and dizzy.

(A bedroom of some sort. Night. The lights are turned out but light from the hall enters to mix with light from a large window on the far wall. ALISON stands in front of the window looking out. SARA sits on the bed, leaning back, looking at the ceiling. They are both holding drinks in red plastic cups.)

(ALISON rolls her head over to also look at the window...)

ALISON. *(inhaling deeply...)* What are you looking at?

SARA. Shhh.

(pause)

ALISON. What are you looking [at?]

SARA. [Be quiet.] I'm having a, one of those, a...

(pause)

It's so beautiful tonight.

ALISON. What?

SARA. Everything.

ALISON. That's what you're looking at...'everything?' How can you look at everything? It's everything. It's, it's...I wanna' go back downstairs.

SARA. This party is kinda' lame.

ALISON. *(laughing...)* I wanna' go back downstairs.

SARA. Fine.

ALISON. And I think we should ditch these guys; there are so many guys down there. Are you coming?

SARA. Huh?

ALISON. What's wrong with you, are you coming back to the party?

SARA. The sky tonight, it's so...vast, it's bigger than anything I could ever even, I mean it's almost hard to look at, like you can't look at it all. All of the shapes [and...]

ALISON. [It's the] sky, you're stoned.

SARA. [Mm hm.]

ALISON. It's actually kind [of...]

SARA. [Yes.]

ALISON. Something [to...]

SARA. [I can] feel my hand, I can feel the veins in it. Rigid. Like wire.

ALISON. Stoned.

SARA. You're stoned. Where did I even get that stuff? I can't remember. It was amazing.

(She laughs. **ALISON** *crashes back down onto the bed.)*

ALISON. What the hell are you looking at? And don't say the sky.

SARA. The neighbors' house, that mailbox. That mailbox across the street.

ALISON. Which one?

SARA. The ugly one.

ALISON. They're all ugly.

(She laughs to herself...)

SARA. Across the street, with the stone swan on top? Oh god. I feel bad for it. Someone knocked its' head off.

ALISON. Good. They'll have to take it down.

SARA. I kinda' like it now.

ALISON. There's no head. It's got no head. Whoa, where did, where did all these bruises come from? I look [like a...]

SARA. [You fell] on the stairs.

ALISON. I fell on the [stairs?]

SARA. [I think] the sky has never looked like it does right now, never in the history of the universe, in all of time, this sky is utterly unique and, and I can stand here and see it and I can hear the blood in my ears. Can you?

ALISON. I think that's just so...so...

ALISON. Can you feel the vibrations from the music? It makes me, when I was little, I'd play records. I actually had a record player, right? Some strange little thing left over from my when my Mom was little. A tiny pink record player for 45's.

SARA. I had a little CD boom box thing.

ALISON. I want to go back to the party.

(She rises and falls to the floor. Starts laughing.)

Oh my God.

SARA. M'are you okay?

ALISON. I'm fine, I just got dizzy, sorta' spinny. And this room is really quiet. You can barely hear the music downstairs.

SARA. This isn't even my room.

ALISON. This isn't your house.

SARA. Right. Right, I know that, I [have a...]

ALISON. [Did] I tell you about, [about...?]

SARA. [It's kind] of dark in this [room, did you...]

ALISON. [You said] to leave the lights off.

SARA. Did I really?

ALISON. I think you, no, maybe I said we [should...]

SARA. [I'm going] to sleep with Charlie tonight.

(She catches herself, covers her mouth. ALISON *points and laughs...)*

I know, I know. He has, I don't know, nothing eyes, easy, kind of still and, well there's not much going on in them, you know? Easy.

ALISON. What about Dave?

SARA. Oh, it's not like I'm gonna' date Dave. He's just fun, he gets it.

ALISON. He's been sending you messages all night.

SARA. He does that when it gets late.

ALISON. Did I ever tell you about my little record player?

SARA. Yes.

ALISON. To play 45's?

SARA. It was pink.

ALISON. Yeah, it was! I would turn it up so loud. That crackling sound would almost cover up the music. That record noise…like a, like a layer of dust on the song. Why Charlie?

SARA. Like someone spilled sand in the music.

ALISON. Why are you going to sleep with Charlie?

SARA. Well he's nice. He brought me to the party.

ALISON. Bad reason.

SARA. It'll feel good.

ALISON. He doesn't look like it would feel good. And I don't like…what's his name? What's the name of the guy who brought me?

SARA. Something. Something like…I can't remember. My face feels like it's [going to…]

ALISON. [I, I can't] stand up. [I think I…]

SARA. [Oh Alison, do] you ever wonder what would happen if you didn't have a face, if no one could look at you and, and, think of all the things you could get away with, that, that would be so amazing, if no one could look at you and see you, really see you and everything was new and mysterious [somehow.]

ALISON. [But you] wouldn't have a face.

SARA. Oh Alison, think of, that's not what I'm talking about! Shut-up, just shut the fuck up, that doesn't even matter!

(pause)

ALISON. I don't feel good, Sara. My head hurts. Everything feels so slow.

SARA. Alison, I want you to tell me the truth. Okay? Really though. Really. Do you think I sleep with too many guys?

ALISON. I don't know. No, not if you want to I guess. Do you like Charlie?

SARA. Oh I don't mean him, I mean all of the...I feel like everyone looks at me like I, I don't, no one looks at me much actually, not at me, you know how people kind of look around you when they're talking, that's better than looking right at you [though if...]

ALISON. [No one] thinks of you as a...

SARA. I don't care anyway.

ALISON. Okay. Well I don't think of you that [way.]

SARA. [All] right. I don't care. I need to go find Charlie. I think he really likes me. He was so sweet on the drive over here. He said we could go whenever I wanted. Whenever I felt like it. And it's not like it even matters if he's good, or I don't care.

ALISON. He, he does seem nice.

SARA. Really nice.

(ALISON reclines on the floor where she fell, stretching. SARA stays at the window.)

ALISON. Or at least not mean.

SARA. Okay what?

ALISON. I can feel the music downstairs.

SARA. I get it. You're right, we should go back down. Do I look all right?

(She takes her purse, opens it, looks at the mirror in the compact, smiles at her reflection.)

ALISON. You look good.

SARA. I do.

ALISON. You do.

SARA. Good. Let's get you up.

ALISON. No, no, just let me lie here for a minute, I can, I can feel the music from downstairs.

SARA. I know, you [said...]

ALISON. [Do you] even remember the name of the guy who brought me here?

SARA. Sure. His name was...his...he was wearing a green shirt. I remember that.

(Pause. SARA crosses back to the window. ALISON is very quiet.)

It's so big out there, like you could just disappear in it, you could wrap yourself up and not be anything anymore, just vanish. Oh, my hearts beating so fast now. And the moon, Alison, are you looking, are you looking? It's almost, almost...

(pause)

Sometimes I wonder if there's anything we can do to, to erase the, not erase but, if there's a way to really change how, I don't know, I can't concentrate but... if we could change ourselves, just a little shift in one direction or the other, that's all, because it seems like everything could be so beautiful, really beautiful if we could just figure out how to see the, focus in on why we so dislike, why we need to, huh...

(She laughs a little, shakes her head as if snapping out of something. ALISON is still.)

I don't even know what I'm talking about. That was... maybe we should head downstairs?

(She does not turn around. ALISON is motionless; her eyes are open.)

Are you still listening to the music? All right. We'll just stay up here, just a bit. I mean, if Charlie's already, if he's gone I can find someone. Guys are so easy, right? I can't get over this sky. Just a...hmmm...

(She sips her drink. ALISON remains still.)

End of Play

snuff film

snuff film was commissioned and produced by Dad's Garage Theatre Company in Atlanta, GA. It opened on January 26, 2006 as a part of *8½ x 11: The Birds & The Bees*. Directed by Kate Warner. With the following cast:

JACK..John Benzinger
JILL ....Alison Hastings
SKIP ....Joe Sykes
TOM...................................... Steve Emanuelson
LAURIE .... Eve Krueger

LIST OF PLAYERS

JACK: a man, a husband, curious
JILL: a woman, a wife, less curious
SKIP: a man, unrequited, all alone
TOM: a man, Laurie's roommate, cynical
LAURIE: a woman, Jack's sister, even more cynical

NOTES

[ ] in the script indicate overlapping dialogue.

The set is three distinct areas in equally spaced spotlights: a chair sitting alone, an armchair and a side table, and a bed and television set-up.

Everything keeps moving, moving, moving; the stage is never still.

(Night. Spotlights up on the three areas. Intense spotlight on the single chair; it is empty.)

*(Normal spotlight on the armchair. **TOM** sits in boxers and a white t-shirt holding his knees to his chest.)*

*(Dim spotlight on the bedroom and perhaps a bedside lamp is on. **JACK** and **JILL** sit on the bed in their pajamas. **JACK** holds a videotape and **JILL** is putting lotion on her arms and legs.)*

JACK. You aren't even a little curious?

JILL. No.

JACK. Well I am.

JILL. That's fucked up, Jack. That is, I don't even, that is just fucked up.

JACK. You don't even what? Know what it is. We should watch it.

JILL. Don't be stupid. Everyone knows those things are all fake.

JACK. Then what's the big deal?

(She looks at him pointedly. She rises and exits into the bathroom.)

What?

*(He sits on the bed and holds the videotape. He sets it down on the bed and lies down on his stomach, face towards the bathroom door, waiting for **JILL**.)*

*(**LAURIE** enters the armchair spotlight speaking, wearing an oversized t-shirt and sweat pants, carrying two glasses of wine. She hands one glass to **TOM** and perches on the arm of the chair.)*

LAURIE. What do you mean you left a letter?

TOM. I left him a letter. I slid it under the door.

LAURIE. Who writes letters? That's the most juvenile thing I've ever [heard.]

(As the scene continues, **SKIP** *enters the single chair spotlight with an envelope in his hand. He is shirtless and barefoot. He hesitantly opens the envelope, removes the letter and reads.)*

TOM. [Well I] didn't wanna' see him. It was weird and I didn't wanna' say the wrong thing or, I don't know. But I didn't wanna' see him.

LAURIE. What's that gonna' be like? A letter.

TOM. I don't care.

LAURIE. I don't know what the big deal is? So this guy spills his heart out all over you. Why can't you just say "thanks, but no" or something?

TOM. I told you, I didn't want to see him again. You weren't there; you don't know how scary he looked when he said it. His eyes were all big and creepy.

LAURIE. Well I think you should be flattered.

TOM. Not so much.

LAURIE. Well…?

TOM. He was scary. Really intense and, I don't know, just scary. And when I told him I didn't know what to say, he seriously looked like he might cry. But in a crazy way. I had to get out of there and today, I thought, well a letter seemed like the easiest way to kinda' handle it. I mean I haven't seen him like that in all the time I've known him.

LAURIE. How long?

TOM. Like, maybe 4 years.

*(**SKIP** leans over in the chair, placing his head in his hands. He crushes the letter a bit.)*

LAURIE. Oh my god Tom, what if he's been totally obsessed with you for the whole time?

TOM. Oh stop it Laurie. Don't [be ridiculous.]

LAURIE. [No, seriously.] What if he's been holding all these feelings in for years and secretly pining for you and wanting you and then, I guess, he finally gets up the courage to say something to you [about it…]

TOM. [Shut-up.]

   (pause)

LAURIE. And you left him a letter.

TOM. I didn't want to see him.

LAURIE. I think that's just sad.

TOM. Yeah, well…

   (Pause. She finishes her wine.)

LAURIE. Oh, I didn't even tell you about Jack? This will make you completely forget about Skip and his puppy love crush.

TOM. Ha ha.

LAURIE. Oh lighten up. It's not like you're the one that got your heart broken.

TOM. What about Jack?

LAURIE. Let me grab the bottle real quick, this is good.

   (She and SKIP rise simultaneously and exit in a similar fashion out of their respective spotlights. TOM swirls the last of his wine and then gulps it down as JILL reappears in the bedroom. She stops at the site of JACK…)

JILL. What are you doing?

JACK. You don't want to watch even a little of it?

JILL. No. Jesus, it's morbid and wrong and it's a little disturbing that you want to watch it so bad.

JACK. Aw, you never wanna' do anything exciting. I'm curious. I wanna' know if this is something people really do [or if…]

JILL. [Don't be] stupid.

JACK. You're being a baby. I'm gonna' put it in.

JILL. No, you're not.

(He crosses to the television that faces away from the audience and puts the tape into the VCR.)

JACK. You don't have to watch if you don't want to watch.

JILL. I don't.

JACK. Then don't.

(There is the sound of static and then noises as light from the television illuminates JACK and JILL. JACK sits on the edge of the bed excitedly; JILL sits further back reluctantly. They watch the tape.)

(LAURIE and SKIP enter again simultaneously, she has the bottle of wine and SKIP still has the letter crushed in his hand. She stops to speak and while speaking SKIP continues to the chair, stops, crushes the letter, takes a step away, turns again, throws the letter down and exits.)

LAURIE. Oh come on. Don't be all gloom and doom.

TOM. Maybe I should have actually talked to him. He [just looked so…]

LAURIE. [Stop that, we're] not talking about that anymore. Now listen to what my stupid brother did, this is fucked up.

(She refills his wine glass and continues as JACK and JILL's faces become more intense in the television light and the faint sounds become more violent, as if someone is being attacked.)

TOM. Okay.

LAURIE. So Jack calls me all excited and just can't wait to tell me about it. He went online trying find some crazy sex thing, I don't even remember [now…]

TOM. [I can't] believe you and your brother talk about these things.

LAURIE. Anyway…he went online and accidentally found one of those crazy movies. Where someone gets killed. A snuff film.

TOM. Shut the fuck up.

LAURIE. No seriously, he found a snuff film and bought it! He's gonna' try to make Jill watch it.

TOM. Jill is never gonna' watch one of those things.

LAURIE. That's what I said, but he seemed kinda' bizarrely excited about the idea.

(SKIP takes a few steps into the light and then exits again looking confused and frustrated.)

TOM. You're right, that is worse. I wish I didn't know that. You're brother is messed up. I don't even think those things are real.

LAURIE. Right? It's totally crazy. All you did was write a letter, so cheer the hell up.

TOM. Okay okay.

LAURIE. Okay.

(As LAURIE and TOM continue, the film gets a bit louder and JILL actually stands up as she and JACK stare in horror at the video.)

TOM. That's such a weird idea. Watching someone be killed.

LAURIE. Or to be excited about watching someone be killed.

TOM. I seriously can't imagine. Who even came up with that idea? Probably someone really lonely. You know, I've never even known anyone who's died.

LAURIE. No one? No grandparents or anything?

TOM. As far as I know, everyone is still alive.

(SKIP enters the single chair light carrying a handgun. He crosses, picks up the crushed letter and sits down in the chair.)

LAURIE. See, now I think that is weird.

TOM. But weird in a good way.

LAURIE. Jack will be fine I bet. They'll probably put in that video and find out it's just some cheap, low budget porn. Or maybe an old episode of Happy Days [or something.]

(They share a laugh.)

JILL. [Oh my] god Jack. [Jack is this real?]

TOM. [That would] [be hysterical.]

JACK. [I don't know.]

JILL. Is this real! [Turn it off, turn it off.]

*(**JACK** is transfixed by the television.)*

LAURIE. [Or maybe some] discolored and distorted version of Sesame [Street. All psychedelic.]

JILL. [Jack, stop it! Make] [it stop!]

TOM. [Jill probably] thinks that's what porn is anyway.

*(They are both laughing as **SKIP** holds the gun to his heart and shoots himself. A spray of blood escapes as his body falls limply out of the chair. The letter is still in his hand. **JILL** screams and slaps **JACK**.)*

JILL. I don't want to see this! What's wrong with you?

*(She exits into the bathroom slamming the door. **TOM** and **LAURIE**'s laughter subsides. **JACK** sits on the bed stunned. He does not look at the video as it continues to play.)*

LAURIE. He's gonna' feel so stupid for spending all that money on a fake tape.

TOM. Well it's better than if he'd actually found a real one.

LAURIE. Sure.

(They sit for a moment…)

TOM. Laurie?

LAURIE. Uh huh?

TOM. Maybe I should go see if Skip's okay. I don't want it to [seem like…]

LAURIE. [Oh no. It's] not your fault he fell for you.

TOM. I guess.

LAURIE. And you said everything you had to say in the letter right?

TOM. Yes.

LAURIE. Then that's that. I'm sure he's fine. It's not like it's the end of the world or anything. He'll be fine. You're not that special.

TOM. Thanks.

(Lights fade on the armchair. Lights fade on the single chair. Lights fade on bedroom, but television light remains up and illuminates **JACK.** *)*

JACK. Honey...? It's okay. It's...

(He is very quiet.)

It's not...not like I imagined.

(blackout)

End of Play

lonesome

lonesome appeared in the annual 10 Minute Play Festival in the Goldberg Department of Dramatic Writing at NYU's Tisch School of the Arts. It opened on December 5, 2007. Directed by Tlaloc Rivas. With the following cast:

RICK . . . . Craig Fitzpatrick
CHRIS . . . . Kaolin Bass

LIST OF PLAYERS

RICK: a man in his 20s, slim and brooding
CHRIS: a man in his 20s, fit and bright

NOTES

[ ] in the script indicate overlapping dialogue.

The play takes place on and around a mattress that's been thrown on the floor of an apartment. Messy sheets. All in a tightly defined square of light.

Outside of the apartment the world is ending.

(Lights up. The light forms a defined square on the floor and the backstage wall; darkness threatening the edges. A window in the back wall lets in a purple-orange light that shimmers a bit.)

(There is a mattress on the floor, unmade, a disaster of twisted sheets. Pillows and bedding are scattered around the room. **RICK** *sits on the mattress in his underwear with his back against the wall. He looks calm, exhausted and his hair is damp and messy.)*

*(***CHRIS*** *enters from the bathroom; he's in a towel.)*

RICK. Ya' know, for a minute, I thought you left.

CHRIS. Can I just say how much I love that shower? There is no shower like that anywhere else in the world. It's really just ridiculous. It's, like, absolutely worth the rest of this place.

RICK. Hey, it's not so bad in here.

CHRIS. Compared to what?

RICK. Out there.

CHRIS. I can't believe you still have running water.

RICK. Luxury, right? I wonder every day if it'll turn dark brown or just be gone.

CHRIS. Well I fucking love it. And the excellent sex, thanks very much. Of course that's both of us. And I mean, it's good to see you too tiger.

RICK. Ugh, that nickname.

CHRIS. Well tiger, it's the one you get. What's so bad about being a big, ferocious [cat?]

RICK. [Chris, I] don't want this to sound, well, I don't really care how it sounds, so…I think you should leave.

CHRIS. I'm leaving, jeez.

RICK. And maybe not come back.

CHRIS. What?

> (RICK *lights a cigarette from a pack lying near him on the floor.*)

Oh nooo[oooo…]

RICK. [What?]

CHRIS. No, no, no. When did you start that shit again? I just saw you [last week.]

RICK. [I don't know,] just couple of days ago if you can believe it. But don't worry; it doesn't matter.

CHRIS. Just, ya' know, you tried so hard to quit; you were such an asshole about it, with the patches and the gum and your temper.

RICK. I don't want to see you anymore.

CHRIS. Where did you even find cigarettes?

RICK. Are you listening?

CHRIS. I'm not deaf. Answer my question. It's, like, impossible to find cigarettes anywhere now.

RICK. Jesus, you are so one track, it's no big deal. One of those looting mobs hit the store on the corner the other day; they were all focused on the owner in the back of the store. I just glanced in and I saw the cigarettes hidden behind the counter. I don't know what happened, but I took them. I didn't think, I just did it.

CHRIS. Whatever man, it's all you. But I wouldn't go near one of those mobs. Those people are fucking nuts.

RICK. You can't come back here anymore.

CHRIS. *(He tussles RICK's hair affectionately.)* There's always a reason to come back.

> (*He leans in and kisses RICK.*)

RICK. Not this time.

CHRIS. *(Laughing it off, he pulls on some jeans from the floor.)* Very serious.

RICK. I hoped I wouldn't feel like this, really, and I know you think you know everything about, um…those are mine.

CHRIS. *(Looks down at the jeans.)* See, I thought they felt a little loose.

RICK. Oh fuck you.

CHRIS. *(He pounces on* RICK, *pushing him back on the bed, tickling him.)* Aww, you don't wanna' share clothes anymore? We used to share clothes all the time tiger. Didn't we? Huh? Huh?

RICK. *(through the forced laughter...)* We used to be in love too.

(Pause. CHRIS, *straddling* RICK, *sits back and stares at him.)*

CHRIS. Have another cigarette or something. What the fuck is wrong with you?

RICK. Look, I'm not, I know we used to be really, whatever, good. And we've been doing this break-up sex thing for a long [time and...]

CHRIS. [I don't] think we can call it break up sex after a year. I think it's just regular sex now.

RICK. Well it's been, I don't know exactly, it feels different. It feels bad. Not the sex, I mean, well, no, it is the sex. It's being with you, being with anyone. I don't want to do it anymore, even the way we aren't together. I can't.

CHRIS. This is better than nothing. That didn't sound right.

RICK. It's like there aren't any rules anymore, it's...it's like a Western.

CHRIS. A Western?

RICK. Everything's like a Western, like some bad cowboy movie.

CHRIS. What does that even mean?

RICK. I don't know. Lawless?

CHRIS. Listen, if you met someone new [then just...]

RICK. [I didn't, I] don't want anyone new; I just want to be by myself. And that's not the same as alone, it's just, look...I never feel more alone than I do right after we have sex. I used to cum and feel it through my entire body, like electricity. I had to close my eyes tight because my pupils spun opened so wide, they wanted to let everything inside my head, like a rush, just this amazing. But now...now when I cum, my body cinches, pulls away; my chest gets tight. I ache.

CHRIS. What a shitty thing to say.

RICK. It's a shitty thing to feel.

CHRIS. Then stop it.

RICK. I can't stop it.

CHRIS. You don't want to stop it.

RICK. Of course I want to! Listen, I'm not being...the cigarettes, when I took the cigarettes? I walked in and picked them up from behind the counter. And there were a bunch of people. I told you, a mob of people, I looked up and I saw them, in the back, around the storeowner. He was on the ground and they were beating him. Not hitting him, beating him. With their fists, with rocks, with anything that was around. And he was squirming a little, just a little. I could see his mouth moving, but I couldn't hear him over all of the yelling. He looked right at me and I didn't do anything. I didn't feel anything about it. I just took the cigarettes and left. I walked out and, just, nothing.

(He takes a long drag off the cigarette.)

CHRIS. Well that's a fucking awful story. Just 'cause everything around us is, like, falling apart or whatever, doesn't mean you have to give in to it.

RICK. I just stopped trying to be something we're not anymore. We're not even people anymore. We're something else now. And it hurts to try to still be the other thing.

CHRIS. Ugh, that's such bullshit. Even though the world ended, and no one's acting like it didn't, it fucking ended, I'm still trying. Things are complicated, things are hard, but that's not inside us, right? That's out there. That's not what I look like inside.

RICK. That's maybe what I love about you most. And probably why I'm so sad when I'm around you.

CHRIS. So you stole some cigarettes, let some guy get beat up, just don't do [it again…]

RICK. [It's not that] I did any of those things, it's that I don't care that I did them; I don't care about any of it. I feel nothing about it.

CHRIS. You're a liar.

RICK. Just get out.

CHRIS. So you can sit around and what? You don't feel nothing, you feel bad. But that's something. And it means you're still you. And all of this other, whatever, is just some pity party. If the sex hurts, then stop having sex, but don't [quit living.]

RICK. [Fucking get] out!

CHRIS. Fuck you!

*(Pause. Stand off. **RICK** collapses back onto the mattress. **CHRIS** slowly sits on the edge of the mattress.)*

RICK. It's so easy, isn't it, to just fall back into it? The sex is easy, the affection is easy and the fighting is so easy.

CHRIS. There aren't that many people out there anymore, it's not like we'll just, I mean you can stop it from fading away, right?

*(**CHRIS** tries to kiss him again, but **RICK** puts a hand on his chest. Then quietly…)*

RICK. When you kiss me, I can feel that man being torn to pieces in the back of that store; I feel every minute of it. I see myself mouthing something I can't hear; then my bones break.

(pause)

CHRIS. Well that's…not real; it's in your head. I'll walk down the street today and see maybe two or three people tops on the way home, right? In a city this size? It all feels pretend. It feels like we shouldn't even be here anymore. But here we are. Here we are. So you don't let it feel that way. It's not bad; it's just different.

CHRIS. *(cont.)* And I know what you feel when you kiss me because I feel it too. But I feel a lot of other stuff that's worth it. And you do too. Look at me. You do too. Because you love me. And I love you.

(Pause. He picks up a shirt and jacket off of the floor, finishing dressing. He gets ready to leave.)

RICK. Chris?

CHRIS. Uh huh?

RICK. Those are still my jeans.

CHRIS. Nah.

RICK. Yep.

CHRIS. I thought, I thought I could just bring 'em back later.

(pause)

So, okay, so…I was so almost out the door. You're such and asshole.

(He strips off the jeans and picks up the other pair, quickly getting them on as he speaks.)

And maybe you shouldn't be smoking. You think? Maybe you should try and appreciate the fact that you're still alive, pretty fucking lucky. Both of us I guess. So fine, I won't be here or, I don't know, I won't kiss you. But you're still a person; we are still people. And we can try to be more than the end of everything. We can at least try, tiger.

RICK. Jesus that fucking nickname.

CHRIS. And just so we're clear. In our little cowboy movie, I'm the lawman. I get the white hat.

RICK. So that makes me the outlaw, the bad guy?

CHRIS. I don't know what it makes you.

(He opens the door.)

RICK. I'm not the bad guy.

CHRIS. You choose that.

RICK. I don't want to be the bad guy.

CHRIS. Then don't.

RICK. This part, right now, this doesn't feel like everything else. I'm looking at you and it doesn't, I'm looking at you. And maybe, maybe you should come back. Just to make sure I'm...still here.

CHRIS. (*He shakes his head and smiles, maybe a little laugh...*) You should have just let me take the fucking jeans.

(**CHRIS** *leaves.*)

RICK. Be safe.

(**RICK** *stretches out on the bed and lights another cigarette. The light box fades leaving only the light from the window to illuminate the area. It moves softly.*)

(*It becomes clear that the light is actually from something large burning. The sounds of people looting can be heard in the distance, people screaming, maybe sirens.*)

(**RICK** *sings a few lines of "Happy Trails" quietly to himself, maybe humming the first bit. He chokes up near the end.*)

Happy trails, to you,
Until we meet again.
Happy trails, to you,
Keep smilin' til then.

End of Play

stop motion

stop motion was commissioned and produced by Dad's Garage Theatre Company in Atlanta, GA. It opened on January 23, 2004 as a part of *8½ x 11: Punk Rock Will Never Die*. Directed by Kate Warner. With the following cast:

ONE . . . . .John Benzinger
TWO . . . . .Alison Hastings
THREE . . . . .Spencer Stephens

LIST OF PLAYERS

ONE: a man
TWO: a woman
THREE: a man

NOTES

[ ] in the script indicate overlapping dialogue.

Should move violently, unapologetically out of control.

(Lights up on **THREE** *with a locking sound. Lights up on* **TWO** *with a locking sound. Lights up on* **ONE** *with a locking sound.)*

(They smile as rock music begins to play softly, almost like a memory.)

ONE. [Live concerts are just the…]

TWO. [I'll usually have straight vodka…]

THREE. [you can see the cut, right…]

(All stop; look at each other humorously, self-consciously. As they begin to speak again, quickly, they also start moving…)

THREE. My lip was bleeding a little. But it didn't hurt.

TWO. Everyone was crushed together.

THREE. The blood looked purple under the lights.

TWO. Hot and sticky.

THREE. I guess it hurt a little.

TWO. [And the band was really…]

THREE. [And the band was really…]

ONE. I go out sometimes. To the clubs.

THREE. For the live shows.

ONE. It's all about being there. Most of the time, I'm kinda' out of the loop. But not when I [go to hear…]

TWO. [An experience.] And I dress for it, but it's not really about [that…]

THREE. [People] think it's [about that.]

TWO. [Trendy] or, I don't know. But no one cares.

THREE. Like you can just look at someone and drop them in their little box with a little label and [a little…]

TWO. [Which is] so [stupid.]

ONE. [Right. So] I go out.

TWO. Not every night, just sometimes. Enough.

THREE. It's not like I have to [go hear...]

TWO. [No, no,] that would be, well something anyway, but I don't have to go.

ONE. I like to go. To be a part of things, experience [the way...]

TWO. [Live and] in person, something [about...]

THREE. [I just] like it.

ONE. It's doing a number on my ears though.

THREE. That ringing.

TWO. The leftover sound, it hangs in the air [around you.]

ONE. [I like to] stand close, I mean really close. So the sweat falls on me, tastes like, I don't know though, my ears hurt even when I have to stand in the back. Maybe it doesn't matter. [Or maybe...]

THREE. [Listen, it's] always loud.

TWO. And that's good.

THREE. Like getting punched in the face.

ONE. Sharper, liked being kicked in the chest.

THREE. Oh fuck yeah.

TWO. Standing in the back, even in the back, like a hammer, no, no, more like a razor. That cuts you, stabs at you.

ONE. More like a blunt razor, that drags.

THREE. If you fight it, so you don't fight it. Why would you fight it?

ONE. But you don't give in either. That's lazy.

THREE. Just change it up some, give a little, get a little.

TWO. You let the music in some, listen to it, [feel it.]

ONE. [And then] it's there, inside you. [And it feels good.]

TWO. [And it feels good] in you.

ONE. Like dancing against someone.

TWO. Slamming into someone.

THREE. Like [sex.]

TWO. [Mmm,] really good sex.

ONE. Throwing someone against the wall sex.

TWO. Violent.

THREE. That kind of [just...]

TWO. [Animal...]

THREE. But it doesn't want [to stay.]

ONE. [It gets in,] it gets in and can't [get out...]

TWO. [Just can't] get back out.

THREE. It wants to [though...]

TWO. [Banging] around, slamming against the inside of your body, all through it, your head, trying to get loose. And you can feel it, breaking things inside, crashing around and, and...you kinda'...

THREE. Like it.

ONE. I like it.

TWO. I like it a lot.

ONE. The music on the outside trying to cut it's way in, the music on the inside is trying to beat it's way out, and I lift up.

THREE. Like you're, like, floating a little in the [fighting.]

TWO. [And] forget.

THREE. I don't have to do [anything.]

TWO. [Don't have] to think of [anything.]

ONE. [Don't have] to feel anything.

THREE. Feel nothing, which is really just feeling too much so it's [like nothing.]

TWO. [Because] sometimes you just want to feel everything, different, even if [it's nothing...]

THREE. [The whole] place buzzes with this group [energy...]

TWO. [You want] to get away from who you are, who other people think [you are in...]

THREE. [You can] feel the other people, smell them, [taste them...]

TWO. [Blank out] the way you feel about yourself. [And the music is...]

THREE. [And the music is…]

ONE. All these things all at once.

TWO. Reverb, coming [at you.]

THREE. [Guitars] screeching.

ONE. Anger.

THREE. Feedback that [hurts your…]

TWO. [Passion] [for the…]

THREE. [Drums,] banging on the…

ONE. Singing.

TWO. More like [screaming.]

THREE. [Yelling,] with that scratchy…

ONE. Pushing!

TWO. Knocking everyone [down!]

TWO. [Laughing!]

THREE. Feeling!

TWO. Really [feeling.]

ONE. [I mean, it's] so many things.

ONE. Escape.

TWO. From [pressure.]

THREE. [From] [responsibility.]

ONE. [Which] [sounds so…]

TWO. [There's a] better way to say it.

THREE. Because it's more like getting away [with something.]

TWO. [It is like] escaping, but not from normal, [everyday things.]

ONE. [From people] telling you what [to do.]

TWO. [And how] [to be.]

THREE. [To let it…]

TWO. And it [gets louder…]

ONE. [And][louder…]

THREE. [And] [louder…]

ONE. [And] [faster…]

THREE. [Oh my] [god…]

TWO. [More] vicious.

THREE. Lashing.

ONE. Beating [against…]

THREE. [Just] [beating…]

TWO. [Then] it stops.

(Pause. Everything stops. They all exhale and then catch their breath.)

End of set. And everyone [screams!]

THREE. [So when the] bottle hit me in the face, [well…]

ONE. [And I] really don't give a damn what's going on anywhere else at that moment.

TWO. *(laughing…)* It's this feeling of, of…fuck you!

THREE. I felt it hit me in the face, but didn't really feel it. Like that.

ONE. Everyone cheers and I cheer with them, all together.

THREE. It felt good.

TWO. And I screamed "Fuck [you!"]

ONE. [And it] only matters for a minute, just that second, [just…]

TWO. [And everyone] around me started screaming it too, and laughing, "Fuck [you!"]

THREE. [My lip] was bleeding a little.

TWO. Everyone was crushed together. And it feels so good, [amazing!]

ONE. [Still] cheering, going crazy when the lights [flicker.]

THREE. [And] then the next band comes out.

(Lights out on THREE with a locking sound.)

TWO. "Fuck you!"

(Lights out on TWO with a locking sound.)

ONE. I like it a lot.

(Lights out on ONE with a locking sound. The music fades in the dark.)

End of Play

swallow

swallow was commissioned and produced by Dad's Garage Theatre Company in Atlanta, GA. It opened on January 21, 2005 as a part of *8 ½ x 11: Live and Uncensored*. Directed by Kate Warner. With the following cast:

JOHN . . . . .John Benzinger

MAN 1 . . . . Steve Emanuelson

MAN 2 . . . . Tim Stoltenberg

LIST OF PLAYERS

JOHN: an attractive man in his early 30s, very confident, almost glowing, but there's something underneath holding him up

MAN 1: the idea of John, a storytelling proxy

MAN 2: a stranger with some new ideas

NOTES

[ ] in the script indicate overlapping dialogue.

The setting for the play is a single chair, stage left, and a large backlit screen.

Man 1 & Man 2 appear behind a screen as shadow figures only.

The sheet that John manipulates throughout the play should have the quality of being never-ending. As John pulls more and more of the sheet onto stage, it should just keep coming.

(Lights up on a chair in spot. Lights fade up illuminating a screen. Two men enter, only their shadows are visible along with the shadow of a bed. They are both laughing, conversing, then begin to kiss, take their clothes off while continuing to kiss and then fall onto the bed.)

(Lights up on the stage as **JOHN** *enters. He is naked and barely covered by a sheet that drags behind him. His throat has a bruise that runs across the front and around one side. He looks pleased. As he crosses to the chair, the sheet keeps coming from offstage; it has no end.)*

JOHN. Feelin' good tonight.

*(***JOHN*** sits, letting the sheet fall over his legs.)*

But that's kind of par for the course, ya' know? Par for the...mmmm...let's not even...

(He laughs, motioning to the screen...)

That's me. But, um...it's not like this happens every night. Don't get the wrong idea or anything...

(He is distracted by watching the screen, tugs up some more of the sheet without thinking.)

Well, whatever idea you want I guess.

(The screen light dims out.)

Whatever you think, that's okay. It's okay, because I love sex. I won't even...And I wouldn't trade anything for sex. Now. Because now it's like nothing you could even imagine, well maybe you could, can...maybe...I mean I'm just some guy, okay. I'm just a guy, regular job, regular car, regular place. Not super-outgoing, even though I'm sitting here like, well, okay...I'm not shy. But I have this, had this, ugh...

(pause)

JOHN. *(cont.)* Sex, how sex used to be, it was, I don't know, I could always almost get there, right? I could do all the things that, the initial stuff. Like really good lines, that eyes across the room stuff, flirting, making out. I'm good at that, I've always been good at that, for whatever reason. Being naked, I love that too. I mean...

(He motions up and down his body pulling more of the sheet onto the stage.)

I really love being naked. I've got the confidence thing, even when I'm uncomfortable, I always find a way to be relaxed. Mostly. My problem, well, it was just the actual sex...Which is crazy, "just the sex," The sex is the most important, I mean that's the whole thing, right? That's the payoff. That's the thing that...I know right, I would get started, that feeling, so good, and almost, I always thought, this time, this time...

But right then it would start, these, I don't know, voices. No, not in a crazy way, not even voices. How do I...? Okay, these feelings, memories of, no thoughts, thoughts kind of hammering around, banging around...I'd be there with this guy and, just, bam! What other people think, what my friends from high school would think, the wedding my Mom always wanted, the way my Dad always asked about girls, the way that my grandparents always talked about how happy I'd make the right lady, the way a family means certain ideas, or, no, not like that, but the way that sex, this, what I wanted, what I was doing right then, was making all of that go away. And, as you might imagine, all of that would put an, um, halt on things.

(Screen light rises, the men are still engaged.)

And it wasn't just some times, that's how it always was, I mean was out, gay in my life, but not, not in, in "practice." Kinda' lonely and disappointed, disappointing. I couldn't figure out how to, how to not, ugh, I don't know...

(**MAN 1** *pulls away from* **MAN 2**, *sits back on the bed and rubs his hand on his head as* **JOHN** *does the same.*)

JOHN. *(cont.)* Until, until okay, this one night, I met this guy, well, I mean I knew him some, I didn't just meet him. But I brought him home and we were, well things were, um progressing and it happened, that inundation of thoughts and worries and anxiety about things that, just, so it happened and I thought, I don't know, whatever I always think, well, mostly just…[I'm sorry.]

MAN 1. [I'm sorry.]

JOHN. But this guy, he didn't just leave. Didn't look down, didn't get mad. He just sat there for a minute, leaned over and said…

(**MAN 2** *leans over and whispers into* **MAN 1**'s *ear,* **JOHN** *whispers…*)

MAN 2. [Have you ever tried choking?]

JOHN. ["Have you ever tried choking?"]

No one leans over and says this. No one just has this in their back pocket, right? But, I don't know, I didn't know what to…

(**MAN 1** *allows* **MAN 2** *to put the sheet around his neck as* **JOHN** *pulls more of the sheet out, puts some of the slack around his own neck and tugs at it playfully, watching the screen.*)

(**MAN 2** *kisses* **MAN** *1 and pulls away tightening the sheet,* **MAN 1** *puts his hands up and then slowly lets them fall away. Begins to rock a bit and then pushes* **MAN 2** *back on the bed.* **MAN 2** *holds onto the sheet.* **MAN 1** *pushes his legs up and they begin to have sex.*)

(**JOHN** *rises while he watches this. The screen dims.*)

Woo! I'll…well, that was it for me, in a second, I was hooked. I never expected, I mean I just thought if I could do something for him, try it, then it would be less awkward, but I never expected.

JOHN. *(cont.)* But I couldn't…just a way to really be with someone else without all of those thoughts, that horrible weight crushing any kind of, I mean, it all just went away, no, it was forced out, drowned out by the sound of blood in my ears, the pounding of my own heart dominated all of the thoughts in my head, all of the sounds in the room all of the things you think when…I could do it, I could fuck. And that's what it was, what it is: fucking. Like I never imagined when, it's incredible.

(A little self-conscious laughing again.)

So now when I, when I do it now, with a sheet, with a rope, now I pull it tighter. Until I think I might explode. I'm sure I look ridiculous or, I don't know. But it's, but it's good in a way, well good doesn't really, because, it's like, okay, I'll try and, okay…

(Screen light rises. **MAN 2** *holds onto sheet around* **MAN 1***'s neck as their activities intensify throughout the monologue, escalating with* **JOHN***'s words,* **JOHN** *uses one hand to hold the sheet tight and lets the other move over his body…)*

When you [pull it tighter…]

MAN 1. [Pull it tighter.]

(The house lights flicker sporadically during the following passage and begin to rise. All lights on the stage also begin to rise. At the climax of the section, all stage and house lights should be at full.)

JOHN. …it's just more, mmm, tighter, and all you can hear is your heart pounding in your ears and all you can feel is the pressure on your neck, tighter, in your chest… and your dick. Tighter. You feel your dick like, like it's your entire, just like your whole body is plugged into your dick, responding like it knows, whatever to feel this way, do anything to, tighter to feel this way and floating, lifting, pushing, pushing, and the pounding in your head, sweat and your eyes pound so you have to close them and you lick your lips, taste salt, knock roaming hands away, tighter, and feel, feel, like, tighter, feel like, everything in between goes away, nothing to distract you, nothing but, nothing, just your dick and the pounding in your head, pounding and it feels so good, slick and hard, so good, like you can, can, like you, you can...[uh...uh...oh, uh!]

(not in unison)

MAN 1. [...uh...uh...oh, uh!]

(JOHN suspends for a minute, like he would float if he could. MAN 1 audibly climaxes and collapses into the bed. All of the lights pulse pack to their initial levels. Screen light dims out.)

JOHN. And then, mmm....

(pause)

Then, then you can hear, no...not the blood pounding, no, this droning, like, like the dial tone, of a phone, only underwater. Then just the breathing, all you can hear is the breathing and everything just slides away, down the back of your neck, your chest, just breathing and these black spots on your eyes where they won't quite focus, and the breathing...

(He shakes it off with a laugh...)

Just, I don't know...but good...so good.

(Screen lights rise. During the next passage, MAN 2 rises and dresses, JOHN continues to pull more of the sheet onto stage, wrapping and unwrapping his hands, toying with the slack.)

I think, well, I think, okay, I'm more intense about it than some people. Even the guys who are into it. It's kind of, I need to do it now. Well that was...blunt. But I guess, I guess I do...it's not as good without the, the added, I don't know, edge. Without that tight kind of pressure that pushes, mmm...Because it takes away the other things, mutes it out and I can, I mean, just enjoy myself. A lot of people don't really get that, get hung up on the idea, but, but it's okay, you know? Everything's okay…

(**MAN 2** *exits.*)

JOHN. *(cont.)* I used to, heh, I used to always think, I mean I'd walk around wondering if people knew I was gay, what they thought, all that kind of crazy shit. I'd kind of self-evaluate: "Does this seem gay?" "How do I look right now?" "I wonder if they can tell?" It really used to just eat me up and that's, I laugh about it now, it seems so…just not what I made it. People are what they are. Now, now I have to wonder if people believe me when I say my eyes are bloodshot because of allergies. Allergies. I have to make sure my collar covers the marks, as much as it can.

It's funny though, in a kinda', well…at the same time, I walk a little taller now. Because I have something that's just mine. A secret kinda' thing.

MAN 1. [Mmmmm and I like it.]

JOHN. [Mmmmm and I like it.]

I'm gonna' try some new things though, new, um, "techniques" right? Because the bruising is getting so I can't really hide it. I mean, a guy has to wear something besides turtle necks and polo shirts. And the headaches, don't even; these dull, throbbing, in my ear and down my jaw…but I wouldn't trade it. Change it, but not give it away. There are other things that you can do, other breath things, rubber balls, plastic bags, all kinds of things and, you can't imagine all of the techniques and, and I'm gonna' try 'em.

(*He collects some of the sheet around himself, rises to exit, turns with a self-conscious smile.*)

It'll be okay, if I keep it up I mean, I should try different things now though because, well, I mean I'm fine, but…it's, it's starting to hurt when I swallow.

(*pause*)

JOHN. *(cont.)* Eh…really, everything's fine. Feelin' good tonight. [Everything's fine.]

(He exits as the stage lights fade. Behind the screen, **MAN 1** *sits up in bed and pulls some of the sheet taught between his hands.)*

MAN 1. [Everything's fine.]

(Lights fade out.)

End of Play

(stereo) headphones

(stereo) **headphones** was developed with actors from the NYU Graduate Acting Program and presented as a part of the Public Theatre Collaboration Lab in the fall of 2007. Directed by Awoye Tempo. With the following cast:

VALERIE. . . . . .Stephanie DiMaggio
SIMON . . . . Matt Carlson
JAMIE. . . . . Nikiya Mathis

LIST OF PLAYERS

VALERIE: a woman in her late 20s, wild hair, wearing pajamas and barely awake

SIMON: a man, Valerie's brother, early 20s, a drug addict, blurring this world with his own

JAMIE: a woman, stylish, a friend stopping by for an unexpected late-night visit

NOTES

[ ] in the script indicate overlapping dialogue.

Valerie and Jamie's dialogue continues to move over the majority of Simon's "rahr" noises. He is largely in his own world for the first chunk of the play.

(VALERIE paces, anxious, clenching and unclenching her fists. She is muttering something to herself incomprehensibly.)

(JAMIE sits in a chair; she looks good, clutching her expensive handbag in her lap. But her posture is rigid.)

(SIMON sits against a huge support pillar in the spare, loft-style apartment. He has on oversized headphones; the coiled cord is wrapped around one of his arms, around his body, leading to a portable compact disc player. He is generally tangled in the cord. Eyes closed, he is lost in music.)

VALERIE. I don't understand.

JAMIE. It was an accident.

(VALERIE stops short and stares at her, stunned.)

What? It was an accident, that's all.

VALERIE. No. Okay, where's the car now?

JAMIE. It's in the driveway.

VALERIE. Under the street light!?

JAMIE. Well what was I supposed to do?

(SIMON laughs a bit.)

VALERIE. Shut the fuck up Simon.

SIMON. There's a tiger in the tall grass. [Rahr.]

VALERIE. [Very] helpful. Jesus I need a cigarette, do you have any?

JAMIE. You know I quit, [Valerie.]

VALERIE. [Perfect] timing, fuck. Fuck. Okay, okay what, exactly, happened?

JAMIE. I don't really know.

VALERIE. You're so calm, I don't, you're so, this isn't like you.

JAMIE. It's just something that happened. And I didn't know [what to do.]

VALERIE. [You came straight] here?

JAMIE. Yes.

VALERIE. You didn't stop anywhere?

JAMIE. No. I stopped at the, no.

VALERIE. Where?

JAMIE. I didn't stop; I just came here. I don't even know why I came here.

JAMIE. You should have washed the car.

VALERIE. Really?

VALERIE. No. No, fuck, of [course not.]

JAMIE. [Valerie,] how was I supposed to wash [the car?]

VALERIE. [In a car wash] Jamie, in a five-dollar automatic car wash. And it was a bad idea anyway.

JAMIE. Look, I just, I didn't want to go home and [I didn't…]

VALERIE. [Was the,] ugh, still, I don't know, alive at least?

JAMIE. I don't know.

VALERIE. How fast were you going?

> *(pause)*

JAMIE. The bumper has a lot of blood on it.

> *(**SIMON** laughs again.)*

> It's not funny!

SIMON. Rahr.

> *(He continues staring at **JAMIE** from this point forward.)*

JAMIE. Can you make him stop doing that?

VALERIE. He's high out of his head; just ignore him. He can't even hear us.

SIMON. Rahr.

JAMIE. Okay, your brother is freaking me out.

VALERIE. You've got a bloody bumper and he's freaking you out?

JAMIE. It was an accident.

VALERIE. Stop saying that, Jesus, please.

JAMIE. What'd he take?

VALERIE. I don't know, whatever he takes. He takes everything. It's fine; he mostly just lies there listening to music.

JAMIE. It's 3 in the [morning.]

VALERIE. [Well we] weren't fucking expecting anyone, okay Jamie, now can we focus on the person you hit? We have to, no, no, you, you have to call the police and report it.

JAMIE. Not a chance.

VALERIE. You don't have to tell them it was you, you can, you can do it anonymously. No one has to [know.]

JAMIE. [You're] right, about the car wash, that makes the most sense. I'll just get the car washed and I'll pay for any damages.

VALERIE. I just, I said the car wash because it was the first thing that popped into my head, it wasn't a suggestion.

JAMIE. No, it's perfect, how would anyone even know.

VALERIE. I know!

JAMIE. Quit yelling, it's not helping. I'm, I'm sure that person is fine.

VALERIE. How are you sure?

JAMIE. Because I am.

VALERIE. This isn't writing bad checks or stealing library books Jamie, you might have killed [someone.]

JAMIE. [No! No,] whoever it was, someone stopped and helped. Someone had to, that's what people do, right? They stop and help.

VALERIE. You didn't.

SIMON. Rahr.

VALERIE. Simon! Okay, okay okay, let's go look at the car, maybe I can tell how bad this [is and…]

JAMIE. [I don't want] to look at it.

SIMON. Tiger, [tiger, tiger, tiger…]

VALERIE. [Fine. I'll go look at] it. Ugh. Don't let him break anything.

JAMIE. Break anything?

VALERIE. Not like, mostly he just lies there, he probably won't freak out. Just leave him alone. Or you can come with me…?

(She exits. SIMON stares at JAMIE. Pause.)

JAMIE. What are you listening to?

(louder)

What are you listening to?

(SIMON is up on all fours. JAMIE is startled and clutches her bag to her chest.)

Oh just forget it.

(As SIMON speaks, he begins crawling towards JAMIE, untangling himself from the headphone cords.)

SIMON. I'm in a field.

JAMIE. That's…good.

SIMON. I'm in a field on my knees in the middle of this field. Really green and grassy, tall grass up around my shoulders and my hands are in the dirt and I can feel all of the little bugs and worms just beneath the surface, really feel them and the grass moves back and forth all around me in the breeze and I hold my head back to look up at the sun, but the it's not there, the clouds are blocking it. And something's wrong with my arm, my arm.

(He gets closer, showing her his arm.)

It's broken maybe, I don't know, sprained or cut or broken, but it hurts all the same, this shooting pain.

JAMIE. Just stay away from me, [all right?]

SIMON. [I can't really] tell what's wrong with it because it's all wrapped up.

JAMIE. [Simon.]

SIMON. [It's tight,] wrapped tight so there's no way to get the [cloth loose.]

(He grabs her leg and pulls her down onto the floor.)

JAMIE. [Stop it!] Get the hell off of [me! Valerie! Valerie…]

(He puts his hand over her mouth, another arm around her neck, and keeps talking, holding her mouth closed, coming unwound.)

SIMON. [I really can't tell what's] wrong with it because it's all wrapped up. Tight, wrapped tight, so there's no way to get the cloth loose. I feel a heat growing on the back of my neck as the sun comes out from behind the clouds, getting hotter, but the cloth's not getting any looser, and I see something getting darker, a red stain starting to bleed through the white. It looks like a bite mark or, no, no that's what it is, a bite, some kind of huge bite mark, and I know I should run, but I can't, my legs won't work, before I can do anything, I have to get this bandage off of my arm. If I can see the mark, I'll know what I'm dealing with, if I can get to the wound, but there's a sound, something sharp, quick, coming fast towards me in the grass and breathing, breathing [heavy, loud.]

*(**VALERIE** enters.)*

VALERIE. [Oh my god…]

*(She rushes towards them and struggles to pull **SIMON** off of **JAMIE**.)*

[Simon stop!]

SIMON. [The cloth is] soaked through with blood, the sound is coming from behind [me, do you hear it?]

VALERIE. [Let her go.] [Let her go.]

SIMON. [She's not] your friend, are you listening, I don't want to, but I turn to see what's coming, so fast, I turn right [as it's on top of me and…]

VALERIE. [Shut-up! Just] shut [the fuck up!]

(She wrenches **JAMIE** *away from him.. **JAMIE** cries out, dragging herself away from the pair.)*

SIMON. [It's right on top of me and I don't] know what to do, I can see it's teeth, can you see her teeth?!

*(**VALERIE** slaps **SIMON** hard, knocking him on his side. He curls up in a ball, clutching the headphones to his ears.)*

VALERIE. Stop acting [crazy!]

JAMIE. [What is wrong] with you?!

VALERIE. What did you do to him?

JAMIE. What?! I asked him what he was listening to and he [just freaked…]

VALERIE. [I told you to] leave him alone. Jesus. You're okay, it's over, you're fine, he's not gonna' do [anything.]

JAMIE. [Like hell.]

VALERIE. He's just fucked up. He wasn't gonna' hurt you.

JAMIE. I couldn't even breathe.

VALERIE. He wasn't going to hurt [you.]

JAMIE. [He could've] killed me.

VALERIE. Oh come on.

JAMIE. He could have killed me!

VALERIE. Well Jamie, he's never left anyone in the middle of the street bleeding.

JAMIE. It. Was. An. [Accident.]

VALERIE. [However many] times you say that, it's not going to sound any better. Don't you fucking get that? It's not okay! God, I need a cigarette, my fucking hands are shaking. Ugh. How are you?

*(Pause. **VALERIE** runs her hand through her hair, pushing it back out of her face. **JAMIE** tears up, drops her head and continues…)*

JAMIE. I…I didn't see her Valerie.

*(The women look at each other. **VALERIE** begins to speak but stops herself. **JAMIE** comes undone.)*

JAMIE. *(cont.)* I wasn't even doing anything, I was looking at the road, I was watching the road but there was so much rain. The radio wasn't even on; I was just driving. And there was this noise, like a, ugh, I didn't even see anything until the noise and then her face was just there, just for a second, I mean only for the quickest flash of, but I saw her face against the glass and maybe her palm, the palm of her hand, her eyes, and then there was another sound and the brakes and my hands. My hands were locked so tight on the steering wheel. The rest of me was floating somewhere else, but my hands were locked so tight…

VALERIE. Did you check to see if she was still alive?

JAMIE. No.

VALERIE. No.

JAMIE. No.

(As **VALERIE** *continues,* **SIMON** *crawls back to his position against the pillar. He is calm again.)*

VALERIE. You have to go back and see if she's okay. What if she's just lying there in the street, bleeding [and…]

JAMIE. [Stop.] Please, I can't.

VALERIE. Honey, you have to go back. You can't not know, and you can't do nothing.

JAMIE. Valerie what if she's dead?

VALERIE. I'll go with you Jamie, let's go.

*(***JAMIE*** looks up suddenly;* **VALERIE** *shakes her head in the affirmative and gets up.)*

Come on, we have to go, give me your hand.

*(***JAMIE*** gives* **VALERIE** *her hand.)*

SIMON. See the tiger's teeth.

JAMIE. What about Simon?

VALERIE. I told you, he's fine.

SIMON. Rahr.

VALERIE. Or, whatever, he'll be fine.

(They begin to exit, but JAMIE *turns to look at* SIMON. *He sits up and looks at her.)*

JAMIE. Did you hear what he was saying? All of that, we he talking [about…]

VALERIE. [I don't] know, are you ready?

JAMIE. I'm ready.

*(*JAMIE *digs her keys out of her purse.* VALERIE *takes them from her.)*

VALERIE. I'll drive.

End of Play

medusa

medusa premiered at Vital Theatre Company in New York, New Y as a part of the Vital Signs Festival. It opened on November 13, 2003. Directed by Bob Cline. With the following cast:

MEREDITH .... Vanessa Shealy
MAN .... Jay Billiet
WOMAN..................................... Jennifer Campbell

LIST OF PLAYERS

MEREDITH – a woman thirties, wild hair, wild eyes, attractive but sad; clearly trying to hang on as much as possible.

MAN – many men

WOMAN – many women

NOTES

[ ] in the script indicate overlapping dialogue.

The two additional actors play all of the ancillary characters in the piece. The initial appearance of each will be noted as (Man) or (Woman), and will then continue with character names only.

(A row of chairs is present, just off center. There is part of a second row visible behind it. The chairs do not look comfortable.)

*(A **WOMAN** enters; she looks rushed, removing her sunglasses to take in the room. She is generally out of sorts. Her hair is in her face. She sets her purse on one of the chairs and two other people, a **MAN** and a **WOMAN**, immediately enter.)*

(They sit, each picking up a copy of a magazine. They read from the magazines, checking in with each other, passing the magazines back and forth, almost gossipy in their interest...)

MAN. The Gorgon sisters were named Stheno, Euryale and Medusa, and [lived in the far...]

WOMAN. [Lived in the far] west, beyond the river of Ocean. Nice. Their heads were entwined with...writhing snakes, [they had...]

MAN. [They had], look, look they had great tusks like a boar, hands [of bronze...]

WOMAN. [Of bronze] and wings of gold, and the sight of them could turn a man to stone. [Stheno and Euryale were immortal...]

MAN. *(exiting with the magazines)* [Stheno and Euryale were immortal,] but Medusa was mortal and [was...]

ATTENDANT (WOMAN). *(picking up a clipboard and pen)* [Mam?] Sorry for the wait. They're ready now, if you...?

MEREDITH. I don't think this is, no, not what I, no...no.

(She pulls out a pack of cigarettes from her purse and move to light one. The attendant grabs them from her, she grabs them back.)

I just need a minute, okay? Just, no, just a minute.

(The **ATTENDANT** *exits. She is left alone.)*

MEREDITH. *(cont.)* Bad habits. It's such an awful thing; smoking. I mean I enjoy it, but that's it then. The thing that's so awful, it's killing me, quietly, everyday, and I enjoy it. And I don't even know if I really do enjoy it as much as I, well, it's harder to not smoke. So I feel better when I do it, as opposed to…

(setting the pack down)

But then that just makes me think about how much power I give to a, to a rolled, well, a leaf. And who wants to be that weak, right? So I quit everyday. Something about cigarettes though, you know? You can quit, anyone can quit. All of our, Peter and mine, my friends have quit, so it can be done. And everyone who quits is so very proud of himself or herself. So proud. But there's something about cigarettes, I know I've said, but unless you concentrate, I mean focus; it's so easy to slip. You can do so well, but stop thinking about it once, just once, and you'll look down and have a cigarette in your hand. And not even know, smoking away and not even realize because it's deeply, no, burned into your behavior. There in your hand, where it's supposed to be. Smoke in your lungs where it's supposed to be. Filling you up a little more, making things, or just taking the edge away. Oh God, it's not that romantic. Trivial. Peter always said, "You really need to quit." I always told him I did.

I never did though. He could be so annoying, get philosophical. Not really, just to bait me. He thought, I don't know, smoking was a symptom of…he would smile at me, bright eyes, and he would say, "Why do you smoke? You know, people who smoke, they do it to fill a need, to [replace something…]

PETER (MAN). *(approaching her from behind…)* [You know, people] who smoke, they do it to fill a need, to replace something they don't have. Something missing. And I never want to think about, well…why do you smoke baby? What is it? What's missing?

(He looks at her expectantly.)

PETER. *(cont.)* What can I do for you Meredith? 'Cause you've gotta' stop. It makes a difference now.

MEREDITH. I have, I quit. No I really, I, I quit.

PETER. You always quit baby...this time you have to stop.

MEREDITH. And he'd put his arm around me and laugh a little.

(**PETER** *laughs a little; a warm, charismatic expression, wanders off.*)

But, but only if we were out, with people, in front of people, so others could appreciate it. He was so...no. He wasn't, but...I'll start somewhere else, okay? Do you, can you tell I'm stalling maybe? Is that...no really, I just need another minute to...My, my sister always told me that Peter was perfect, that to her, he was perfect. She was perfect, Sara. I have two sisters, older, Sara and Elizabeth. They are, it wouldn't be fair to try and, they're honestly untouchable: beautiful, strong, above everything. But not in a negative way, more removed, I would say, from anything difficult or plain. You'd call it grace if it were that simple. It isn't though; you can't learn it. You have to have it...I never had it. Let me just, I was always pretty, or, please don't think that's, ugh...I mean I always had confidence, but never that thing, that quality. It was like they floated, and nobody could reach them, unless they chose to come down. So when Peter asked me, when he came up and asked me...I lifted up. Right in front of them, I lifted up into his arms. And they were smiling, my sisters... but all of the other women there looked at me like...I was the vulnerable one. They looked at us together, Peter and me, with this...their faces had this quality that I can't, or don't want to...we were married young. He was twenty-four, I was twenty-one. Not so young I guess. We'd been married for a year before I found out he'd been after both of my sisters before me. They both turned him down, which is my luck it seems. He couldn't catch them, but he caught me. I was, no, the vulnerable one. Or I wanted to be caught.

(She takes a pill from one of the bottles, then another from another bottle, then some water.)

MEREDITH. *(cont.)* I'm not; they said not to take anything. I can't see how it could hurt really, when the whole point is…if you're not supposed to take anything, why do they let you have it? I mean, I brought it with me, but they've seen it. I'm not making any effort to hide the pills, the bottles, any of it. No effort. And everyone walks around like I'm not even here.

(She shakes the bottles in the air looking for a response from someone.)

Like, no, it' not like that, but I want it to be like I'm not…No effort. But that's not exactly, no, unusual for…I mean I have trouble finishing things. My attention tends to wander after any kind of, like I can't concentrate on things, bring them into focus. That doesn't make any sense, does it? I wasn't always, everything was so…clear. Now I am like this. This, my thoughts don't seem to stop anymore, just speed around and everything seems more intense. But also distant or…blurry? I don't know.

Do you ever watch the Discovery channel?

Bear with me all right? I had never watched the Discovery channel. It just doesn't seem entertaining, right, like anything educational automatically loses its' entertainment value. 'Boring' I'd tell you. I'm more network, mainstream, ya' know? So one day I'm flipping through the channels, looking for, I don't know, it doesn't matter. I see this man in a cage. No, in a wet suit, in a cage, being lowered into water. I thought, huh, "what the

Hell is this?" I mean…I kept flipping, but it came around again and these men were throwing chunks of, handfuls of blood and just, flesh into the water around the cage. This is not something that you run across, have you seen this? This man in the cage, okay, these people are out on a boat, out in the ocean trying to study sharks. And this man climbs in a cage and allows the others to throw bait into the water in order to attract sharks, so he can see them up close. So he can, what is going on in this guy's head? But of course, no, of course they have a camera in the cage and I stopped flipping through the channels. I couldn't even remember what I was trying to watch at that point. As soon as the camera was underwater, there's a moment where I couldn't tell much, and then clearly, in this nightmarish fade, just enough light to see sharks everywhere. These gigantic, and just, just going insane. Banging into the cage, biting the cage, bending the God damned bars, jarring the camera around. A blur in the water, thrashing and…it wasn't even a picture, just an idea: violence.

(pause)

MEREDITH. *(cont.)* And there's the voice of this man, the man in the cage, narrating in a voice over. 'The beauty of [these creatures…']

(She sits in one of the chairs and a soft light illuminates her. Another area lights up in bluish light and a **MAN** *appears.)*

SHARK WRANGLER (MAN). [The beauty of] these creatures, really, is to see their power and efficiency when roused to action. Most shark Species are in danger of extinction due to a pervasive fear, hunting and poaching, but most of all, commercial fishing. Huge dragnets designed to pull up marketable catch haul everything in their wake for miles. So the fishermen are after the smaller, more viable fish, but they catch the sharks just the same. Today, we have endeavored to find a highly populous area. Upon arrival, my colleagues have dumped large amounts of chum into the water in order to attract as many animals as possible. The goal here is to observe the sharks in a frenzy situation. With the help of this camera, we can [capture the true nature…]

MEREDITH. [What is wrong with] these people? Get out of the damn water!

(The lights drop on the **SHARK WRANGLER.***)*

I was actually screaming at the television, at these people risking their lives for nothing. What he learned from that was really never clear to me, or I didn't understand why it was important to know... I just didn't understand. But good old Discovery channel, they won a viewer that night, a loyal viewer. Which is sick in its' own way really.

(She reaches for a cigarette, then catches herself and pushes it back into the pack. Laughs a little.)

I don't know what made me think of that just now. Anything to pass the...interesting anyway. And don't get me wrong. It was not always that exciting...in fact, well, hardly ever, but it was worth it for the truly captivating moments. Of course once you see something like that, it's indelibly etched on your brain. Images that you can't get rid of no matter how hard you try. All you can do is...hope to forget.

There was this one special, a documentary, on gorillas. I've seen it four times now. About that woman who actually lived in the jungle and, I don't know, 'communed' with the gorillas. She earned their trust and they took her in, let her live with them on a daily basis. And that's all it was really, all of the gorillas living their lives. It's fascinating, how much like us they are. People say that and I think "sure, sure"...and then you watch them and, well, you just don't expect to suddenly be confronted with this...

There's, okay, there's this one moment, about three-quarters of the way through, they show this mother carrying around her baby. The thing is though, that the baby isn't moving. It's not...it's dead. It's not alive anymore and she just keeps dragging it around with her...like she doesn't know. I couldn't watch that part, but I couldn't not watch it when...and every night now, I have this dream that I'm the mother gorilla in that show, in the jungle. I see the cameras from the Discovery channel and I want to show off my baby, so I nudge him and lift him up, but he's lifeless. He just lies there and I feel it...I know how it must feel. I know why she doesn't let go, why she keeps pulling him around everywhere, trying to feed him, trying to play, trying to anything, anything...I wake up crying and Peter always tries to give me pills. I never take them, not the sleeping pills. I mean I do, I take them all the time. All the pills: blue, red, white with little pink writing. Anything to make it go away. So I'm not, you see, I mean I take them, just not when he gives them to me.

MEREDITH. *(cont.)* It's...I like the Discovery channel fine. I like it well enough, it's entertaining and...I guess that was the point. Oh God, I don't give a damn about the show. I get a little, don't worry about, I get a little. Ha? I sound like Sara. Sometimes I [get a little...]

SARA (WOMAN). *(collapsing into one of the chairs)* [Sometimes I] get a little faint is all. You're so sweet to worry, but don't, really; you know how it is.

MEREDITH. You look tired Sara.

SARA. Well thanks little sis. That's always nice to hear.

MEREDITH. It wasn't supposed to sound [like...]

SARA. [Meredith,] don't be so serious.

(She offers a smile.)

I am I guess, tired, all the time now. Between work and the baby, all the crying and feeding and changing, it never stops. She just never wants to sleep. It's so much harder than I thought to juggle everything and I, oh... oh honey, I didn't mean to...you know I wouldn't... Meredith?

MEREDITH. This happens, this moment. All the time! People don't forget. Anyone who tells you that people will forget something if you give them long enough has never needed people to forget.

*(**SARA** exits, **MEREDITH** follows her to the edge of the stage while speaking.)*

MEREDITH. *(cont.)* My sisters love me, my friends, the friends I still talk to, but sometimes I think they are too careful. It's like they have to navigate a conversation with me, to avoid any missed steps. And it really shouldn't be like that. It never used to be, not unless we were fighting. They never fight with me now, not even when I go out of my way to provoke it. Trust me when I tell you this: I can be terrible when I try. But no one will engage me, like they're walking on glass. I actually, uh, I go out of my way to pick fights with strangers. Anyone, people on the street, people who don't know me or know to be so damn careful. I want someone to yell at me, scream, get in my face, push me, shake me, lose control and, and…something, just something. I want it. I have never been a nice person. Pleasant, but not nice. You wouldn't know it just looking, from the outside. I was that girl in high school, in college, that you hated probably. The one who had everything and knew it. Flaunted it without having to try, effortless. Happy. The one who acted just so and was still somehow…cold. I'm her, that's me. Effortless. And boy did I a lot to learn. About wanting, about…really needing. That's, I don't know, maybe a bit harsh. I have a, a tendency to remember things with a slant. But we all do that I guess. I had friends that were close, I did, no, I wasn't that bad. I wasn't. And my sisters were there for me. Even though I clearly felt apart from them, my sisters were always there. They taught me a lot about being a girl, then a woman. I looked up to them so much. So much. In fact, if I had a daughter…

(She stops.)

It's so easy to…no.

(She crosses, takes several pills, a long drink of water.)

I don't give a damn. They said it might be bad, for me, bad for me if…how could it not? What the hell does that mean? Just…fuck.

Oh fuck.

(Pause. Collects her things into a pile on one of the chairs. Sits for a moment running her hands through her hair...)

MEREDITH. *(cont.)* I had a son. We found out early on, or I guess as early as you can, that it was a boy. We decided on Patrick after months, literally months of arguing. Day in and day out...Michael, Jonathon, Jacob, David, Jeffrey, Chase. Chase, I loved that name for a boy. Peter hated it. He said we should save it for next time; maybe we'd have girl. We were actually in the delivery room and still didn't have a name for sure. But we'd talked about Patrick, passively agreed on it as a solid fallback, if it came down to the wire. And it did. I think childbirth is the most painful, well that's not an original observation, but it was so...even more than, but it was quick for me. An hour, in that respect, I was lucky. I had a son. Peter was with me in the delivery room. I thought my head was going to explode, I mean, my body had already been ripped, really just, but it was my head spinning and this pressure that was pulling me up and pushing me down all at once, all at once. And then it was over, just nothing, heavy breathing and, just, exhaustion. Through the sweat and the hair in my face I could see him. Peter squeezed my hand and I...the nurse held him and said, "Congratulations. [Here's your son...]

NURSE (WOMAN). [Congratulations.] Here's your son. Look little guy, there's your mommy. There [she...]

MEREDITH. [And] Peter wiped some of the hair back and kissed me on my forehead. And I looked at my son. He was moving a little, just a little, and it was this beautiful moment, I remember thinking, this is everything. I finally have, but...I noticed, he was so quiet. It wasn't, no, he was just very quiet. And the way she was holding him, he was looking right at me, as much as he could, and I was looking at him.

(pause)

MEREDITH. *(cont.)* He stopped moving, it was this horrible stillness. I felt like I was watching everything in slow motion, slowing down in front of me, this gradual winding down, but it wasn't, it was so fast, everything. So fast. She said, "Look little guy, [there's your mommy."]

NURSE. [Look little] guy, there's your [mommy, there she...]

MEREDITH. [No, no,] she said, "Doctor, [there's something wrong."]

NURSE. [Doctor, there's] something [wrong. He's...]

MEREDITH. [And she] turned away, [kind of...]

NURSE. [I think you] should [look...]

MEREDITH. [She, and,] and I [couldn't see...]

NURSE. [There's something] [wrong with him...]

MEREDITH. [She said] she said, ["Doctor! He's not breathing!]

NURSE. [Doctor! He's not breathing!]

MEREDITH. I felt, no, my body shake, but in a detached way, like it wasn't my body, like floating. No! No, like the Ocean, when you're in the ocean. How the water lifts you up a little and then knocks you around. So there's no real balance, it's hard to find a footing and the waves are cutting through you. Beating you back, pushing you...I passed out.

(A lengthy pause then a deep breath as she crashes back into one of the chairs.)

It's, I think, I don't remember, but I think that I never, just didn't want to wake up again. I knew. But I did, I awoke to this sound I had never heard before, to Peter crying. He looked at me, really looked at me for the first time ever. It hit me all of the sudden how he never looked in my eyes, right into them, right then. I wouldn't look away and he couldn't look away, couldn't move. I almost didn't hear the doctor, that's ridiculous, of course I heard him.

DOCTOR (MAN). Mr. and Mrs. Rook, [I'm so sorry.]

MEREDITH. [I'm so sorry.]

DOCTOR. Unfortunately, your son was, he had a physical complication, a deficiency, underdeveloped lungs. There's really no easy way to do this. I…after the labor, he didn't have the ability to, not enough oxygen was [reaching his heart…]

MEREDITH. [Reaching his heart.]

DOCTOR. …and as a consequence…He had some shallow breathing, but he was not able to, we weren't able [to save…]

MEREDITH. [Don't!]

(*pause*)

So I had, he was alive, even if it was only for…so, so we had to sign the birth certificate. [Patrick Ashley Rook, born to Peter and Meredith Rook on December 2nd at 5:43 AM.]

DOCTOR. [Patrick Ashley Rook, born to Peter and Meredith Rook on December 2nd at 5:43 AM.]

NURSE. [Died December 2nd at 5:50 AM.]

MEREDITH. [Died December 2nd at 5:50 AM.] Seven minutes…he had seven minutes. And he was so beautiful. After it was over, I came home and stayed in bed for a week. Not, I don't mean that to sound, I did actually stay in bed for a week…maybe longer. And still I think that it felt like years. Empty…adrift. I sound so, no…Peter took care of me, in a walking dead sort of way, but he handled everything. And we didn't look at each other. Some things, I don't know, force people together, out of need or desperation, to get through. Not for us, not at all. Our house was so quiet. And he was so very still, standing…in the hallway, in the doorway, in the dark asking me, quietly asking me "Do you need [anything?"]

PETER. [Do you] need anything?

MEREDITH. And I would say, "I'm fine."

(pause)

PETER. I…all right.

MEREDITH. And that is how we were. My sisters came by, did their best. Now I know that, at the time I didn't care. My body ached, my heart was twisted into this, this knot that…nothing in life prepares you for that. When I finally did get up, okay, laying in the bed I didn't think about anything. Nothing. Memorizing the sounds the house made or listening to the clock ticking until it's all I could hear. But that's no way to, day after day. Standing in the shower a week later, water hitting my neck, running down my back, it all crashed in on me like, like the sky was falling. On me, all of it landing on me. Crushing my insides. I started crying uncontrollably, shaking, just lost it. Curled up into a ball on the floor of the shower. I stayed in there for, I don't know, an hour maybe. Maybe even… When I finally climbed out, dragged myself out really, the bathroom was all fogged up and sticky. I hate that, you know? So I wiped the mirror clear with my hand and saw myself, through the streak, really saw myself. I looked…my hair wet and in my face, my eyes blood shot from crying, dark circles, pale and exhausted. I looked so, and I, I…I realized I this is how I must have…I realized that this was the only thing my son got to see in his entire life, me looking like that. His mother like some kind of monster. He couldn't breath, he couldn't even cry, move, all he could do was look at me, like that…what an awful, oh God…

(pause)

This place. It's like an amplifier for whatever you're feeling. Well, for the bad things, all of the dark things that you try to, try to forget. Why do I need…? Ugh…I hate this place. No. I hate, I just hate…Something inside me is not right. And I think maybe, in some way, that this is my punishment. My fate or…but I don't even know what I did, really I….

(She reaches grabs the cigarettes and puts one in her mouth, catching herself, she throws the pack and cigarette on the ground, recoiling.)

MEREDITH. *(cont.)* Fuck. I can't go through it again. If something happened, I wouldn't be able to, Peter wouldn't. So I'm here. Is that wrong? Peter, he wants to try for another child. We still can, the doctors said if we want. We can if we…but I can't. I told him I would, but I just can't. He thinks we just have bad luck; that I'll get pregnant again eventually. He does have bad luck. He has me. And I'm weak, and I'm frightened, and I'm sad…and I lie.

(Pause. She places her hand on her stomach lightly…)

That's why I can't keep this one. No, none of them. I don't want to go through it again, if it…? No more chances, no more tries.

ATTENDANT (WOMAN). Mam, I'm sorry, I know how difficult this is, but they won't be able to wait any longer. You'll need to come with me now if you're still going through with...

MEREDITH. I'm ready. I'm, no…let me just…I'm ready.

ATTENDANT. After the procedure, we'll bring you back here to rest up [and...]

MEREDITH. *(packing up her bag, picking up the cigarettes…)* [I know.] I've…I've been here before. Bad habits. There are worse [things…]

ATTENDANT. [All] right then, if you'll just follow me...

MEREDITH. I can do this again…

ATTENDANT. I'm sorry?

MEREDITH. Nothing. Nothing.

*(Pause. The **ATTENDANT** goes on ahead, she falls into one of the chairs. **PETER** enters, dragging, tired. He sits in one of the chairs across the stage, flips on an unseen television with a remote control. Lights up on a **TELEVISION ANNOUNCER**, the same bluish television light from earlier.)*

ANNOUNCER (WOMAN). But Medusa was mortal and killed by Perseus. He found the Gorgons asleep, and by averting his gaze, and looking only at [their reflection...]

PETER (MAN). [And by averting his gaze], and looking only at their reflection in Athena's [shield of polished bronze...]

ANNOUNCER. [In Athena's] shield of polished bronze.

PETER. He couldn't see her.

ANNOUNCER. He averted his gaze.

PETER. Couldn't look [at her.]

ANNOUNCER. [Wouldn't] look at her.

PETER. Shield of polished [bronze...]

ANNOUNCER. [Polished] bronze, he cut off [Medusa's head.]

PETER. [He cut] off Medusa's head. She had been...?

ANNOUNCER. She had been pregnant by the sea god Poseidon at the time.

PETER. She had been...

ANNOUNCER. Yes.

PETER. She had...?

ANNOUNCER. Yes.

(He jerks to shut off the television. Lights out on the **ANNOUNCER.** *Lights fade off* **PETER.***)*

MEREDITH. So one more time then. I can do it...and you'll never have to see me. Never have to look at Mommy. I can do it. I'll never have to, I want...just a look, I need it, no...no, I can do this. One more...goodbye.

(blackout)

End of Play

Also by
Steve Yockey...

Bright. Apple. Crush.

Cartoon

Octopus

OTHER TITLES AVAILABLE FROM SAMUEL FRENCH

BRIGHT. APPLE. CRUSH.
Steve Yockey

Drama / 2m, 1f / Bare Stage

Three monologues intermingle, each character explains what drove them to murder. One man set fire to his house after finding his wife cheating on him in their bed. A woman (a teacher) gives poison apples to all of her students because she just can't stand them anymore. Another man, physically abused by his lover, ultimately crushes his head in with his boot.

Published in *Off-Off Broadway Festival Plays, 32nd series.*

OTHER TITLES AVAILABLE FROM SAMUEL FRENCH

CARTOON
Steve Yockey

5m, 4f / Comedy / Unit set

Join the exploits of a band of mismatched cartoon stereo-types on a wild ride through this animated world, Presented in the style of a Commedia dell'Arte scenario gone berserk, Cartoon is a devilishly violent social commentary that explores the rapid coalescence of media, politics and consumer giants. A young, idealistic upstart named Trouble steals the giant hammer that Esther, the bratty dictator, uses to maintain a monotonous but peaceful order. Chaos ensues. Bombs explode. Puppets are set free. Anime girls fight. And as the bodies pile up, the violence begins to creep off the stage and into the audience. There's nothing like a punch in the face to really get the blood moving.

"Fast-paced, funny, and drenched in pop culture. If you see only one play about cartoon characters killing each other this year, make it this one."
- East Bay Express

"Yockey's piece plays like an Eastern European communist-era political comedy, with farce and cruelty artfully intermingled to create horrifying situations... whose frequent leaps from cartoony cuteness to over-the-top violence are both shocking and hilarious."
- LA Weekly

"Cartoon poses profound questions with every laugh...it will leave you thinking and discussing the play for the remainder of the evening."
- Backstage